Set in a rural southern town, Lynchburg native Rodney Syler's Yellow Fever reminds the reader of the pure fun of imagination-fueled childhood adventure. It's a nostalgic tale, of Don, Ray, and Amber as they navigate their friendship and the rural county looking for treasure and a sense of belonging. It's an engrossing story of resilience and the power of childhood friendships. It's Home Alone meets Treasure Island with a small town southern twist.

–The Lynchburg Times

YELLOW FEVER

FINDING THE TREASURE WITHIN

RODNEY SYLER

ARCHWAY
PUBLISHING

Archway Publishing books may be ordered through booksellers or by contacting:

Archway Publishing
1663 Liberty Drive
Bloomington, IN 47403
www.archwaypublishing.com
1 (888) 242-5904

ISBN: 978-1-4808-9198-2 (sc)
ISBN: 978-1-4808-9199-9 (e)

Library of Congress Control Number: 2020911461

Print information available on the last page.

Archway Publishing rev. date: 07/16/2020

For all those kids—young and old—who feel trapped and unable to get out of their current circumstances. Get wrapped up in the possibilities of this story, but know that there is a way up and out in real life. Seek the help of others. Be willing to give up an environment that keeps you in a circle of bad behavior or bad results. This is a work of fiction, but there are so many real stories where, in what seem like dead-end situations, people persevere and are triumphant.

Following is a list of books and articles which contain stories of real people who came from tough situations and found a way to make lemonade from lemons. See also the list of helpful organizations.

Downs, Annie F., *Perfectly Unique*

Downs, Annie F., *Let's All Be Brave: Living Life with Everything You Have*

Zuckerman, Gregory, *Rising Above: How 10 Athletes Overcame Challenges*

Ackerman, Susan, *Reno Rising: You Have to Fall Before You Rise*

Wilson, Pete, *Plan B: What Do You Do When God Doesn't Show Up the Way You Thought He Would?*

Shallenberger, Rob, *Conquer Anxiety: How to Conquer Anxiety and Optimize Your Performance*

The Bible: The Book of John (If you want a good place to start)

Street, Elizabeth, "Overcoming Obstacles: What Oprah Winfrey Learned from Her Childhood of Abuse"

Organizations

Men of Valor, Men's Christian Centered Prison
Ministry, Nashville, Tennessee
Oasis Center, Nashville Tennessee, Crisis Number
615-327-4455 (24/7) www.Oasiscenter.org

DEDICATION

I would like to dedicate this book to my wife Lisa who has always stood by me and believed in me no matter what I attempted. She is a big part of my Treasure Within.

Additional thanks to all the others who read and re-read drafts and endured my fledgling attempts to be a novelist.

There is more treasure in books than in all the
pirates' loot on Treasure Island...
—Walt Disney

1

Burn Center, Nashville, Tennessee

Fourteen-year-old Amber woke up to searing pain and blinding light. A hand went to her forehead and another to her wrist. "Stay calm. You've been through a lot."

"I remember the fire and the smoke. Where's my little brother?" she whispered.

"You've been sedated for a week. You are burned badly across your torso and back. You have extensive skin grafts. It's going to be a long, difficult recovery, but you can do this."

"How's my brother?"

Three months later, late spring 1975

Amber's mother shuffled into the hospital room. Lisa had not been in the fire, but her gaunt face and hollow eyes hinted at something equally bad.

She brought Amber an old shoebox tied with a bow but instructed her to open it later. Then her mom presented a ragged, stuffed teddy bear. It was ancient and heavy with the weight of sawdust stuffing. Lisa said the little bear had been handed down through generations, and now it was for Amber to pass the valuable heirloom to her children. According to her mother, the box and the bear were her future.

The tattered bear reminded Amber of her own gauze-covered burns. Both the bear and Amber had topaz eyes. Though the bear's eyes sparkled brilliantly, they were no match for the fire of determination in her eyes. Smart and strong, she was ready to get on with life, a better life.

Amber asked, "Why give me this stuff now?"

The other shoe dropped. Her mom said, "Amber, you are strong. I know you are just fourteen, but you are much stronger than me. I can't take this anymore. The drugs, the fire, my son, it's all killing me. I'm leaving tonight for Mexico. You will be okay. I love you so much."

Amber tried to speak, but no words came out. Her mother kissed her goodbye and struggled to the door. In the hallway, she sat in a wheelchair, and a nurse pushed her away.

Lisa had tried to shield Amber from the truth. Terminal cancer forced her to seek last-ditch treatment in Mexico. As the wheelchair disappeared down the hall, Amber wondered if she would ever see her mom again.

Later, her face wet with tears, Amber resolved to get on with her life. She remembered the wrapped box. Inside the shoebox were baby clothes, a tiny hospital armband, notes, and the most recent letter from her grandfather who went by his last name, Preston. The bottom of the shoebox was stacked end to end with bundles of hundred-dollar bills. Amber knew she was on her own when she saw the money. It was time to test her self-confidence. Emboldened, she did an hour of stretching and exercise, showered, and then waited for the physical therapist to take her to the gym for her last session.

Within two weeks, police told Amber her addict stepfather was a suspect in the devastating house fire. Her world was falling apart. Rather than becoming a ward of the state, she put her plan into action. She showed her stepfather the letter from her grandfather, which invited her to come to the farm. Amber told him she was taking a bus to be with Preston for the summer, and maybe forever. She stuffed a backpack with the shoebox, the bear, and the things she had salvaged from the fire. With a few clothes in a travel bag, she made her way to the bus terminal.

It was early summer, late on a perfect afternoon, when the Greyhound lumbered to a stop. She thanked the smiling driver as he dragged her bag from the cargo bay. Amber stepped behind the bus and inhaled deeply. Coughing from the fumes and wiping her watering eyes, she laughed at her mistake. She was looking so forward to the cliché "breath of fresh country air" that she had nearly gagged on diesel fumes. Only later, when she was closer to the farm, did she appreciate the scents of hay and blossoms. She strolled leisurely the remainder of the mile toward her grandfather's farm, enjoying every minute free from the hospital and the city. Skirting the locked driveway gate, she followed the gravel drive.

Amber made herself at home. She crawled into an unlocked window and retrieved her bag from the porch. The house smelled musty and brought back memories of home-cooked meals and Old Spice cologne. After a tour of the house and confirming that Preston had indeed left the farm, she was pleased to see the power was on. Amber finished a candy bar from her backpack and looked around for more food. The remaining food was mostly canned. She saw sugar and flour but nothing perishable. The refrigerator was empty except for ketchup and an opened jar of pickles.

Soon night darkened the room. Amber decided not to use the lights since no one knew she was staying there. After a brief entry in her diary, she undressed, pulled the covers to her chin, and instantly fell asleep in the four-poster bed.

Amber's diary entry: "Free ... clean country air ... a little scared ... I can do this."

Amber was on fire again! She jerked awake to the smell of smoke. As she tore at the covers and rolled to the floor, she expected to feel the heat and the burns. Fear and panic consumed her. She looked around for the flames. Instantly alert, she slipped into her jeans to escape the fire. It was so dark. She scrambled to the open window to make her escape, only to realize there was but a faint smell of smoke. There was no sign of flames.

Settling down, she took a few deep breaths, removed her hand from her scarred chest, grabbed her flashlight, and toured the house. Everything seemed in order. Nothing was burning.

Amber returned to the unfamiliar bedroom, turned off the flashlight, and gazed into the darkness. It was her first night truly alone and on her own. As she reflected on her long bus ride into the country and arrival at her grandfather's abandoned farm, she noticed a flicker of light in the nearby woods. Could it be a campfire? Had the campfire smell drifted into her room and morphed her dream into a nightmare? It seemed so real. This was the first smoke she had smelled since fire had consumed her bedroom. Almost burning alive in a house fire, made her very sensitive to the smell of smoke. Now she was wide-awake and curious. No one was supposed to be on the farm—not even her.

Slipping into her high-top Converse tennis shoes, Amber decided to investigate. Taking the flashlight and one of her grandfather's walking sticks from a bin by the door, she crept in the direction of the woods.

Leaving the flashlight off, Amber's night vision was good enough for her to navigate the yard.

Once through the gate and across the small pasture, she angled toward the tiny flicker. Her feet and legs were wet with dew as she stopped in a rocky creek bed to listen.

Amber tracked the blaze through the trees. The voices were louder as she inched closer, creeping silently in the dew-covered leaves. Amber crouched behind a log and listened. Two boys threw sticks into the fire, making sparks rise high into the treetops. The sparks winked out only to be replaced by the glitter of stars in the clear night. The boys' backs were toward her, but she could make out their profiles as they turned and told their stories. It was apparent they were telling ghost stories from phrases like "headless horseman" and "blood everywhere." Big hand gestures and bobbing motions accented the storyline as the bigger one's long hair bounced about his shoulders. The smaller, bespectacled boy was on the edge of the log, more standing than sitting. Even in the dark, she could sense his fear as he stole glances into the woods.

Amber observed a small tent, sleeping bags, and even an old iron skillet propped near the fire. Concluding they were there for the night, she had a mischievous idea. While she closed her eyes and waited for her night vision to return, one boy said, "Every time you tell that story, you make it seem like a headless horseman is galloping right through our camp."

The other boy said, "That is because the story is true. Headless horsemen show up when the night is clear and there are just enough stars for the horse to see."

Amber carefully slipped back out of the woods. At the small creek, she put down her walking stick and flashlight. Carefully feeling around in the dark, she gathered a half dozen rounded rocks about the size of walnuts. Though yards away from the crackling fire and raucous ghost story, she still moved soundlessly to avoid detection. Amber decided to add a bit of special effects to their ghost stories, like a throw to home base from center field.

She had played softball the summer before and had quite the arm. For three months after the fire, Amber attacked the weights in physical therapy. Having to endure the pain anyway, she embraced it and made the best of the program. She accepted the pain as she stretched the scar tissue and became stronger and in better shape than ever.

Two rocks in quick succession ripped through the leaves ahead of the boys in the darkness. The story stopped and was replaced by frantic chatter. Since the boys had been looking at the fire, their vision was compromised. They could not have seen Amber if they had looked in her direction. Now, the two boys were standing with their backs toward her. Aiming to the right this time, Amber sent two more rocks into the trees. More cracking branches and loud agitated voices followed as the boys tried to make sense of the noise in the trees.

Deciding the boys were scared enough, she pocketed the last two rocks, retrieved her flashlight, and ducked quietly back across the field to the house. Going inside without any lights, she felt her way along the wall to her bedroom. She took off the damp clothing and climbed back into bed. Content, she drifted off to sleep, thinking the two boys might not sleep at all.

* * *

The next morning, the boys were awake early. Their sleep was fitful, waking to every tiny sound of the forest. They added wood to the remnants of the fire and pulled some hot coals to the side for a pan of bacon. Ray dumped two pounds of meat into the skillet and stirred it with a stick.

These were local boys, raised on the farm next door. Because their farm was mostly open fields and row crops, they did their camping on Preston's place. Preston did not mind. The boys had been a big help over the years.

Preston gave them the run of the farm. He asked them to keep an eye on the place while he was gone. They even had a key to the gate and a long string of numbers to call him collect if there was anything suspicious. The boys could hardly believe he had gone all the way to Australia. The female veterinarian he met and ran off with was quite a lady. Once they started going out, nothing else mattered to Preston. He was head over heels.

* * *

From the campsite, the aroma drifted over to the farmhouse. The smell of bacon in the morning woke Amber with a smile. Suddenly realizing she had slept late, she slipped out of bed and put on her denim shorts and Converse. Pulling a sweatshirt from the bag, she noticed a wisp of smoke from the woods, but she could not see the tent or the boys.

After thinking about the previous evening, the boys in the woods seemed familiar. Two years ago, she had spent part of the summer planning adventures and playing with them. She remembered one of them had crudely repaired glasses. Though she only saw silhouettes by the campfire, she was quite sure the mysterious campers were Ray and Don Spark.

She went to the kitchen and looked through the cabinets. There were jars of honey, peaches, jelly, and things she did not recognize. She opened a can of peaches, forked out the big pieces, scarfed them down, and drank the juice out of the can. Peaches were good, but she could not forget the aroma of the freshly cooked bacon.

* * *

Ray poured grease into another pan and fried some eggs. He stirred a bubbling skillet of gravy. Don grabbed a bag of leftover biscuits from his pack and dished up two plates from the skillets on the fire. After breakfast and scraping out the skillets, Ray brushed the knots out of his shoulder-length hair and stretched his lean body like he was reaching for the treetops. He and Don were having growth spurts, and stretching seemed to make everything feel better.

While Don put away his sleeping bag, Ray went for a walk.

Ray decided to look around and check on Preston's house and barn. When he got to the edge of the woods, he could see a fresh path through the tall grass. Following it to the creek bed, he saw one of Preston's walking sticks on the rocks. He looked back toward the house and had an idea that someone might be meddling with Preston's stuff. That same someone might have messed with them last night! Thinking there could be an intruder; he grabbed the walking stick and made his way back to camp.

Don was getting the camp in order, and Ray explained what he had found. They hatched a plan to find out who was messing with Preston's place.

It could be robbers or bad guys who had been near their camp. Before they alerted the sheriff, they decided to get a closer look. Building the fire bigger to make it look like they were still at the campsite, they slipped through the middle of the woods to the back of the farm. Passing the sharecropper house near the river, they approached the barn and the house unseen.

As they neared the back of the barn, Ray went to the corner and peeked around. There was nothing in sight and no movement. They slipped into the barn loft for a better view.

Don noticed movement in the house. A dark shadow dashed across the kitchen, and Don said, "Ray, there is a burglar in the house. We better go home and call the sheriff."

Ray said, "I want to see the intruder first."

Don and Ray had always been curious. Thinking they might get a better look from the shed, they ducked out of the barn. From behind the tractor, they had a good view through the open kitchen door. Someone was in there. It was a girl. She was looking away, but she was definitely a girl. With shorts and a sweatshirt and dark red hair all puffed out with big curls, she looked really familiar. Don and Ray looked at each other and smiled.

Two years ago, they had met her. In fact, they had spent part of the summer getting into mischief together. Ray and Don had talked about her often. To them, she wasn't Preston's granddaughter; she was a goddess. They had not seen her in two years, but they had fantasized about her and elevated her in their minds to goddess status.

Now here she was, not seventy feet away, light shining across her through the doorway, the edges of her hair like fire in the sunlight. She turned, as if she knew she was being watched and stared right at them. They could not move. Her face broke into a broad smile as she marched straight to them. She remembered who they were and the great fun they had two summers ago.

Amber held out her hand. "Hello, I am Amber Preston. Remember me? I can't believe how you two have grown."

Both boys were speechless. Ray recovered first and said, "You dropped your walking stick." He smirked as he handed her the sturdy hickory staff.

* * *

Sitting at the kitchen table, she told them Preston had invited her to spend the summer there. However, she admitted, there was a problem.

He had gone to Australia, and if certain people found out she was there alone, they might call Child Protective Services and have her taken away. She explained about her stepfather going to jail and her mother's sudden trip to Mexico.

Neither Ray nor Don spoke.

Amber said, "You are probably wondering how you can help."

After a few seconds of silence, Ray said, "That was exactly what I was wondering."

Amber said, "We could start with some bacon I smelled cooking—if there is any left. I am starved."

The dew had dried, and they trekked across the field to the camp. After bacon, cold biscuits, and three Dr. Peppers, their friendship was renewed. No one had any idea what adventures and challenges would come from this friendship. For the remainder of the summer, they were rarely apart. Even though Don was a year younger, they were all going into the ninth grade. They were fit, smart, precocious, and an exceptional team.

As they laughed and joked around the fire, no one was in a position to see the old truck with a camper creeping past the driveway gate.

2

A few days later, Amber heard a truck in the driveway. She knew the gate was locked. The truck drove past the house and backed up to the shed where Preston's tractors and mowers were kept.

Two scruffy men with dirty clothes and beards looked around suspiciously as they positioned two ramps. The men checked to see if either riding mower had a key. Realizing the danger, Amber glanced at all the keys hanging by the door. Next, she guessed, they would be coming into the house. Though it was not quite dark, she waited until they looked toward the house to turn on the porch lights. They took a step back toward the truck. Amber wondered if they would think the lights were on a timer. She did not want them to know a kid was staying alone in the house. It didn't occur to her that being female might be an even bigger problem.

While she waited, she took a picture through the blinds of the men and their truck.

One man made a show of shouting at the house. "Hey, Preston, we're here to get the riding mower for service. Where's the key?"

Amber flipped on the eve lights and moved upstairs for a better view.

The two strangers ran back to the camper, threw the ramps inside, and sped away.

Amber took another picture of the back of the truck as it bounced past.

* * *

The driver growled to the passenger, "He said no one was home—and he would buy anything we could haul. I told you he was a double-crossing liar."

"Maybe we need to slip back in here tonight and see if someone is home. There is too much stuff to walk away without being sure. If he doesn't pay us like he said, we will have to make a midnight visit to his big fancy house."

* * *

Amber's heart raced. She had a feeling they would be back. When she walked up the driveway to the gate, it was still closed and locked. However, there were tracks to the side where the truck drove around. She decided it was time to make an impression!

The gate blocked the road, and a deep ditch made the creek side impassable. However, on the other side of the gate, the grass was wide enough for the truck to drive around. Amber went back to the shop and turned on the lights. She found some boards in the corner and looked around until she found a hammer and nails.

After driving the long nails through the boards, she flipped the first board over to examine her work. She silently thanked her grandfather Preston for teaching her to use a hammer. The nail points were about two inches through the boards. Amber made a few more spiked boards and loaded them in the tractor bucket. After locating a shovel, she drove to the entry gate.

The recent rain made the ground soft. By the tractor headlights, she dug just under the grass and flipped the sod over beside the trench. She placed the boards, nails up, in the shallow trenches and replaced the sod carefully to avoid the spikes. In the flickering light, it looked menacing. The next unwanted visitors would be very surprised.

Amber went home satisfied with her work. She crawled into bed, fully clothed. Lying still atop the covers, she was ready in case the scruffy characters in the pickup truck came back.

Amber's diary entry: "Discernment … That is what I need right now … Be brave."

At two in the morning, she woke to a noise on the road. A vehicle passed by the entrance slowly, but it kept going. Moments later, it returned and slowed at the gate. A loud pop sounded as the truck drove onto the spikes. Then a shriek rang out.

A few minutes later, she heard the truck start again and rumble slowly down the street away from the farm. Proud of her night's work, she smiled in the dark and drifted off to sleep.

Amber woke the next morning to sunshine coming through the window. She didn't even know when she had gone to sleep. Maybe the satisfaction of beating the bad guys again had helped her get some rest. She got ready and ate a relaxed breakfast. Belly full, she was anxious to get to the road and see what kind of damage her nails in the board trick had done.

She drove the tractor out to the road, and as expected, there were more tracks. This time, they stopped short. Some of the boards were overturned, and one of the boards looked as if it had been thrown to the side. Amber looked closely and saw blood on the spikes and smears of blood on the board. She realized the nails did not stick in a tire. One of the bad guys must have stepped on the nails and punctured his foot. She decided to take the board with her. The blood sample and the pictures might come in handy someday if she needed to get the sheriff involved.

Amber went back to the shop, parked the tractor, and walked back in the corner where three-sided shelves were built into the wall. She remembered checking for eggs in the nests on the shelves, but now they were adorned with pieces of junk, oilcans, and oily rags.

Pushing all the debris aside, Amber put the bloody board on the top shelf as a souvenir. She remembered her satisfaction from the night she scared Ray and Don by the fire. She fished the two remaining smooth stones out of her pocket and placed them on the shelf with the spiked board. That would be her trophy case—a memory place.

A good feeling spread over her. She did not fully understand the feelings that had started a few months ago. Though the pain of exercising to stretch and develop her injured body was terrible, an internal feeling gradually came to balance and eventually overpower the pain. Now was one of those times. Warmth grew within her, a feeling of pride and accomplishment, like a power she was discovering. It felt so good. At times like this, she almost forgot about the pain of the burns—and she almost forgot about the hurt of being abandoned—but she did not forget the memories of her little brother.

She was startled by a noise behind her. Afraid it might be one of the thieves, she turned with the nail-spiked board in her hand.

Ray stepped back. "Amber, it's me. What are you doing with a weapon?"

A little embarrassed, she put the board back on the shelf.

Ray wanted to know the entire story. When it was over, he said, "Do you think they will be back?"

"I don't know. I don't want to have anything stolen. Before we tell your dad, how can we discourage people from thinking the farm is easy pickings? Let's get with Don, put our heads together, and come up with some ideas."

They met near the cave at the picnic table by the river. It was a perfect early summer day, and the river was almost silent as it drifted past. An occasional sound of someone far away on the river floated through the silence.

From the top of the picnic table, Amber looked up through the trees.

Ray and Don were on the two benches. They understood their great fortune to have such freedom. Some of their friends had to work in the summers. They, too, would eventually get jobs, but for now, they had freedom.

Don wanted to do some hiking in the woods and insisted they plan while they hiked. Everyone agreed and headed into the woods in search of adventure. They talked as they walked, and Ray suggested a game.

They saw a tall hickory sapling, and it reminded him of something he had seen on an old Tarzan movie. "In the movie, natives from the jungle captured some explorers. They pulled down tall treetops with ropes and tied their captives between two trees where they were stretched or pulled apart. They called it Juju."

Amber held up her hands, shook her auburn curls, and said, "Not for me. I've been through enough torture for a lifetime."

Ray explained how his version was different. All three kids would climb the hickory tree until it reached the ground.

Amber said, "How do you know the tree won't break?"

Don said, "Hickory is known to bend really well. As long as there are no limbs, they will bend almost in half."

Ray said, "It will be like a ride at the fair. We bend the tree down, two people let go near the ground—and the other one is launched into the air!"

Don said, "That sounds like fun!"

Amber said, "If I do it, I'm wrapping my legs around the tree so I don't fly off into the sunset.

With the plan in place and everyone willing to try, Ray climbed the tree, closely followed by Amber and Don. As they approached the limbs at about twenty feet, the tree began to bend. They continued a frenzied three-way dialogue as the tree groaned and bent. Soon, all three had toes touching the ground. They looked like clothes hanging on a line. Ray wrapped his legs around the tree trunk and held on like a monkey.

Amber and Don let go on the count of three, and Ray held on tight. The tree accelerated up, and as Ray was pulled skyward, he yelled with delight. He went past the center and swung far to the other side before the tree eventually righted itself.

Ready to take their turns, Amber and Don climbed back to the top of the tree. This time, as the tree bent toward the ground, it was Amber's turn to be Juju. She wrapped her legs around the trunk, and the boys let go. She launched up and over the top as the tree swung past center and then recovered to vertical. Amber was thrilled to be having fun again.

Still high in the tree, Amber said, "Ray, this was a great idea."

Don and Ray shimmied up the tree as Amber was climbing higher to make room. As the tree bent near the ground, Ray and Amber released their grip before Don had his legs around the tree. He catapulted skyward. With his legs hanging down, a squeal sang out as he accelerated right out of his denim shorts. While he swung to the opposite side of the tree, underwear like a white flag, his shorts fluttered down onto the top of a nearby bush. As Don swung back and forth in his underwear, high in the tree, Amber and Ray laughed hysterically.

Amber took out her Instamatic camera and snapped a picture. Shaking the nearby tree and bushes finally brought Don's shorts to the ground. A little embarrassed, Don slid down and retrieved his shorts. He would have been humiliated had it not been so much fun.

Amber said to Ray, "Remind me to put a belt on his Christmas list.

After the Juju, they headed back to the picnic table to eat snacks and make plans. Amber and Ray agreed Don definitely got the most style points for his ride. They decided adventure would need to be a part of everything they did. Making a pact, they agreed to do their best to make life a big series of adventures and to hold each other accountable.

3

Their first order of business was securing the front gate. Even though the boards with nails had worked, they decided it was too dangerous and might hurt an innocent person. After considering alternatives, like adding a fence or digging a ditch, they settled on bringing in a big rock. The biggest rocks were high on the bluff, inaccessible to Preston's tractor. They took pry bars with them to loosen a big rock and slide it or roll it down to the open area near the cave.

Amber announced a lunch break before they started. They made peanut butter and jelly sandwiches and drank chocolate milk. Taking a few minutes for lunch to settle, they debated how big the rock should be. They decided the bigger, the better. If they could move it down the bluff—and the tractor could manage to pull it to the gate—then they would have the perfect rock. One large, well-placed boulder would stop almost any car or truck.

Ray brought the tractor close to the cave and parked it. He was most familiar with the terrain and led the hike up the zigzagging path to the top of the bluff. Most of the trip was on all fours, clawing to keep from falling back or sliding off. They towered about one hundred feet higher than the cave at the top.

Along the way, they saw many rocks. Some were solid ledges and would not budge. Others were too small. More than once, they pushed a big rock only to watch it slide, roll, and sometimes bounce high as it went toward the bottom. Most rocks stopped short and hit trees along the wooded bluff. Along the top of the bluff, there were several good choices. The first one they chose was about the size of a double kitchen sink. They pried it onto its side and gave it a shove. It flipped, bounced, and rolled the wrong direction toward the river. It finally splashed into the water after knocking down a few tiny trees.

The next choice was much larger. It was about ten inches thick and almost as big around as a small kitchen table. It was already on its side on a steep slope. It looked like it would not go toward the river if they could get it on its edge. The three of them pried and wedged rocks under the upper side. As the rock angled higher, it moved more easily. In order to get it to roll like a giant wheel, they had to rotate it. As soon as it was nearly positioned correctly, Ray pushed on the lead edge and slipped as the rock began to roll. He scrambled to the side as the boulder gained speed rolling past him. They watched as hundreds of pounds of solid rock gained momentum. Barely missing trees, it went faster and faster. It bounced over ledges in the bluff and was airborne by the time it was halfway down.

Amber said, "Look at it go!

The boys' excited faces went slack as they looked beyond the boulder.

Far below, the tractor was in the direct path of the plummeting rock. It hit a tree about ten feet above the ground and exploded right through it. The treetop fell sideways as the boulder accelerated down the bluff. To their horror, the boulder hit the ground like a big wheel. Still increasing speed, it made a direct line for the tractor. There was a log on the ground near the tractor. As the boulder hit the log, it went airborne. The tumbling boulder barely scraped the hood as it flew across the tractor. It rolled up the embankment on the other side of the lot, then slowly rolled back toward the tractor and toppled over.

They all stood amazed. The power of gravity on the boulder was much more than any of them had imagined. The tractor could have easily been crushed. Thankful they had achieved their goal and destroyed nothing in the process, they laughed with relief.

With a chain secured around the rock, the tractor puffed dark smoke as it pulled the rock toward the entrance. Fitting perfectly in the middle of the grass beside the gate, it looked good and made a statement.

Another security measure Amber tackled alone was hiding her cash. She found the root cellar under the house. It was dug about seven feet deep into the dirt. Steps were carved out in the dirt with old boards across them for shelves. Though all sorts of produce like apples and potatoes could stay down there for months, only about a hundred assorted jars remained. Amber found a space below and behind everything else, took most of the cash from the shoebox, and divided it into six blue quart fruit jars. She kept some spending money to put under her mattress, and packed the jars into the hiding place in the ground.

Later, Amber looked through the shoebox her mother had given her. Among the scraps of paper and letters was a faded scrap with strange barely visible handwriting. She thought it was written with one of those fancy calligraphy fountain pens until she realized it was much older, maybe written with a quill and ink. The lines were smeared with ink spots; the style of writing was very formal. Only a portion of the letter remained. The edges were torn or had been worn away. A few phrases were legible: "come back for it" and "back door to the round room." The first name was torn away, but the last name of the signature was clear, Preston CSA.

Amber heard two sets of "hoo hoo hoo" in the distance and then silence. Amber, Ray, and Don had worked out a signal. Since Amber wanted to keep her presence a secret from authorities, Don had suggested an owl hoot as a distant greeting or warning. Two sets of three meant Ray and Don were on their way over. One set of three, in return, gave the all clear to come on in. Three sets of three meant danger!

Amber returned the "hoo hoo hoo" and soon had company. Ray and Don were staring over her shoulder at the paper from the shoebox.

Amber said, "My mother gave me the box before she left for Mexico."

She showed them the tiny bracelet she had worn as a newborn, some letters from her real dad before he was killed in Vietnam, a picture of him in uniform, and a Purple Heart in a tiny box.

Don lifted the old scrap of paper and handled it carefully. "This is really old ... I mean really old. Who is it from?"

"All I can make out is 'Preston CSA,'" said Amber.

Don's eyes twinkled with excitement. "CSA is the Confederate States of America. The Civil War was from 1860 until 1865, over a hundred years ago. I didn't know any of Preston's people were in the Civil War. I wonder who he was. What else does it say?"

"Most everything is difficult to read. It mentions two strange things. 'Back door to the round room,' and 'come back for it.'"

This got Don and Ray excited. They loved a mystery.

Don said, "Maybe we could find out which of Preston's ancestors was in the Civil War. I bet it is in the library."

"You're the genius," said Ray. "If anyone can find out, it's you."

Amber said, "Can you check for a family tree? I would help with some of this research, but I have to keep a low profile for now."

In the afternoon, Ray and Don went to town with their mom, Britney. She dropped Don at the library, and Ray went to the grocery. He bought some things for Amber with money she had given him. He put bread, milk, cereal, butter, orange juice, some personal items, and a dozen cokes in a cardboard box and closed it. When he put it in the back of the car, his mother did not even seem to notice.

When they stopped at the library, Don was ready to go. He could hardly keep still on the way home. Once out of the car, they grabbed the box and started toward the woods to see Amber.

Their mother stopped them and asked, "Are you boys ready for supper?" When they began making excuses, she said, "Have you heard of mother's intuition? Let's have a look in the grocery box."

Ray and Don looked at each other and then at the box. Out of choices, Ray put down the box and opened the top.

She said, "Camping supplies I suppose?"

The boys nodded vigorously; relieved their mother had provided the perfect answer.

She flipped through the articles in the box. Near the bottom, beside the gallon of milk, was a pink hairbrush!

"Have you lost your brush?" she inquired with a knowing smile. "And have you acquired a preference for pink?"

This was a tough one. With his shoulder-length hair, a brush could be explained, but a pink one?

Seeing his dilemma, Britney again came to his rescue. "Or was pink the only color available?"

Ray smiled as if she had the right answer.

Britney said, "I took a walk earlier today and thought I should check and make sure Preston's farm was okay. He did ask your dad and me to keep an eye on things. Can you imagine my surprise when I saw you and Don walking right inside and make yourselves at home? Later, the prettiest little auburn-haired young lady walked you both out onto the porch! I have been wondering if maybe you two have been spending some extra time over there. In fact, once I thought about it, I have hardly seen you two for the past week. Would the pretty young lady happen to be Amber Preston?"

"Yes, but we can explain!" said Don. And he did. As he ended his explanation, he said, "Amber expected someone would eventually find out. And this fall, she will need to get into school. Her main fear is a report to Child Protective Services."

Britney listened without interruption. "I think it's time I met with her myself. When your dad gets home later tonight, we will talk to him too."

The groceries went back into the car, and they drove around to the gate.

Ray went down to the creek to retrieve the hidden key from under a ledge.

Britney said, "I don't remember seeing that huge rock there before. It looks nice."

Ray and Don smiled with satisfaction.

Ray closed the gate behind them, and they drove to Preston's house. It was nearing dark, but no lights were on.

Don put his hands to his lips and whistled like an owl. Two sets.

After a brief pause came the simple reply: "Hoo hoo hoo."

Amber turned on the porch light and walked out.

Ray, Don, and their mom came to the porch.

Amber said, "Hello Mrs. Spark. I suppose you know I am Amber Preston. Please come in. We should probably talk."

Mrs. Spark turned to Ray and grinned. "Don't forget your box of camping supplies."

The house was neat and clean. The bed was visible through the open door and was neatly made. No dirty dishes were in the sink.

"Amber, would you tell me what exactly is going on and how I might help? I know a little about your family and the fire. It was awful from what I read in the news. The paper reported your mother left not long after the fire and your stepfather was indicted and awaits trial on charges. You, according to reporters, are in the custody of your grandfather, Preston. Since he is in Australia, and you are here, I wonder if maybe you could use the help of an adult."

Ray and Don were very proud of their mom.

Amber retold her story and admitted that, although Preston had invited her to stay for the summer, he did not know she was here. Though she fully intended to stay, she did not know how to register for school, especially with her grandfather out of the country.

The four of them talked for an hour and devised a plan. Britney Spark composed a letter to Preston with a proposal for Amber to stay there and enroll in school. Amber wrote a supporting letter about how she was keeping the farm in good shape. Both Mr. and Mrs. Spark agreed to check on Amber daily and act as guardians in his absence. If he would agree to everything, there were a few documents included for him to sign to ensure Amber could attend school in the fall.

In her letter Amber told Preston that she had money to care for herself, and she would make sure the farm and house were kept perfectly while he was gone. Then she simply asked Preston to please let her stay.

When Ben Spark got home, he was supportive but amazed. He had been gone for a week, and they had all but adopted a troubled girl about the age of his sons. Since they had it all planned, he agreed to "see what happens."

4

Don burst into Amber's living room and jerked to a stop as he saw Amber and Ray leaning in nose to nose across a small table. A surge of jealousy instantly came over him as he stared at her quivering back. Neither of them reacted to his entry as moans came from the couple. Stepping to the side he instantly felt foolish as he saw both their red faces straining in concentration. Amber leaned in closer and with a guttural growl, slammed Ray's arm to the table.

Panting, Ray said, "That was just a practice round. Next time we arm wrestle, I won't be so easy on her."

Amber laughed and Don said, "Looked like you were trying pretty hard to me. Maybe you should start exercising like she does."

Ray said, "Did you come running in here just to give me a hard time?"

Don said, "Before Mom got involved and we got busy with letters to Preston, I was planning to tell you what I discovered in the library."

As they walked to the kitchen table, Amber said, "Don't keep us in suspense. What did you find?"

"I researched military volunteers from the county and found two Prestons who had volunteered to fight for the Confederacy in the Civil War. Checking the newspaper stories, I found one of them was killed very early in 1861. Nathaniel Preston, however, was a quartermaster and served throughout the war.

Amber said, "What is a quartermaster?"

"They are in charge of getting supplies and equipment to the soldiers. Nathaniel was decorated and given secret missions to advance the war effort. It was rumored he had been in charge of moving cash and payroll money around the South to keep it out of the hands of the Union soldiers. Nathaniel was Preston's great-grandfather or great-uncle. It is difficult to be for sure. And he was raised right there on this farm!"

Amber said, "I didn't realize this house was over a hundred years old."

"It's not," said Ray. "There is an old rock foundation closer to the river. This house was built around 1900. And I bet you remember the stories about the other house—the sharecropper house!"

Don said, "Amber, what were the two phrases in the note in the shoebox?"

Amber retrieved the box and opened the note, and Don told them the story he had read in the library. "Apparently, many people believed that money and gold disappeared near the end of the Civil War. People were getting shot and lost in battle all over the place, and communication was terrible. Payments would go to troops, and many had nowhere safe to put the money. Money probably got lost, and some was buried for safekeeping. Some of the soldiers did not live to come back and recover it."

Don suddenly realized what he was saying. He remembered Amber's real father had gone to war and died in action, never coming back for her. Turning to Amber, he said, "I am so sorry. I didn't think."

Amber had tears in her eyes because she had made the connection too. "It's okay. It's been a long time. You didn't mean it to be hurtful. Go on with the story please."

"After the war, Nathaniel never came back. Everyone thought he was lost in battle. About sixty-two thousand soldiers died during the war."

"What is your point?" asked Ray.

"There was a rumor around the turn of the century suggesting that Nathaniel brought the money here and hid it. Several stories were printed about men coming here and nearly destroying the place, digging mostly in the cave. The original cabin is gone because somebody burned it down while looking for money."

Ray said, "How stupid. If they burned the cabin looking for money, they would burn the money. And Confederate money is worthless anyway. I've seen it in museums."

Amber said, "Maybe they were looking for coins. Maybe they were even looking for gold."

Don said, "The confederacy started making some of their own coins, and they had some gold. However, even if gold was here, and we found it, there would be problems. Some people would claim it belongs to the soldiers' families or to the government. Somebody would want the taxes. I have read stories about shipwreck treasure where they spent thousands of dollars to recover gold, and everything went to another country."

Ray said, "I think you are counting your chickens before they hatch. We have heard of people looking for gold in the cave, but why here?"

Don had a terrific grin on his face and ticked off the reasons on his fingers. "One, because he knew this farm inside and out like us; two, because he was in the area; and three, because I know where to find the gold!"

Amber looked at Ray, and they both looked at Don. "Where is it?"

"The clue is in the note." He held it high. "Back door to the round room. Come back for it."

The clues fell into place for Ray, but Amber was in the dark. Amber said, "What is the significance of the round room?"

"You would not know unless you explored the cave. You still would not know unless you had the scrap of paper with the clues. Now we have both," said Don.

Ray explained, "The cave down near the river goes back into the hills under the bluff. It is easily accessed near the river, and people go in there frequently. Preston posted, a sign but people still sneak in. It doesn't have many formations remaining intact. American Indians probably used it for shelter. There is also an Indian mound in the woods near the cave."

Amber asked, "What is the round room?"

Don said, "Not too far into the cave, there is a passage leading into an almost perfectly round room. People go there all the time."

Amber replied, "If people go there all the time, then the money is probably already gone."

Ray said, "People have certainly searched all inside the cave. Not everywhere, of course, because there are centuries-old piles of boulders and breakdown. There is graffiti and names all along the low ceilings and walls. Most are made with soot from carbide lamps or candles. Some mention treasures or gold and X marks the spot."

"Are there any from the Civil War?"

"Yes, some look authentic, but many are fakes," Ray said. "I'm pretty sure the ones reading, 'U. S. Grant was here' in green spray paint are not genuine."

Amber said, "Don, why are you so sure you know where it is?"

"I know because there is no 'back door' to the round room! There is only one way in. We need to find a passage leading like a back door to the Round Room."

5

Early summer rain was falling, but it did not affect their plans to go into the cave. They each had a small pack with flashlights, candles, a lighter, candy bars, a package of spare batteries, and some rope. Britney knew they were going in the cave and what time they would be out. They did not tell her why they were exploring. The cave was a cool fifty-six degrees inside, and they dressed in layers. They moved in a line with Ray in front and Amber in the middle. After about fifteen minutes and only one crawling passage, they came to the Round Room.

It was almost round, had a dome ceiling, and was about twenty feet across. The dry ground was covered in shoe and boot prints. It was the most visited room in the cave. Don and Ray searched every inch of the back wall. There were some gouges in the limestone from picks and chisels, but there was no sign of an opening.

Amber took out her sketchpad and added to the sketch she had started as they entered the cave. While the boys scoured the cave walls for clues and gave a running commentary, Amber counted and sketched. Palming a small compass in her right hand, she made a note on the sketch.

Ray came over to look at the detailed sketch of the cave section they had traveled. It was simple, but it showed passages, steps between prominent features, and directions by the compass. According to her sketch, they were about three hundred feet into the hillside and about two hundred fifty feet from the river's edge.

She said, "Let's go out of the room and take only passages leading back in the direction behind the round room."

Searching those passages was not very helpful. Most went the wrong direction. They returned to the round room entrance and stopped for a snack.

Don suggested checking every square inch of the main passage as it led away from the round room. Floor to ceiling, they examined everything they could reach. They looked close and far, but they found no passage.

About a hundred feet beyond the round room, Ray stopped. He noticed most everywhere there had been a side passage, the ceiling was different. Channels in the limestone, dissolved thousands of years ago, branched off in the direction of the side passage. Ray said, "What if we look for the signs of a side passage rather than the passage itself?"

"Worth a try," said Amber as she went back to the round room entrance. Observing the channels, she moved down the passage with her light on the ceiling. She stopped forty feet from the round room. Some of the channels in the ceiling were perpendicular to the main passage and disappeared directly into the stone!

The three of them stared at the wall. It looked like all the other cave walls: solid rock or layers of dirty limestone. The ceiling was flat, about ten feet overhead. At about eight feet over the floor, there was a slight offset, blocking visibility above a tiny ledge.

Amber said, "Don, you are the smallest. We can lift you for a closer look at the top of the wall."

Don scrambled onto Ray's back, and Amber steadied the duo. It was not the stuff of cheerleading fame, but it got Don near the ceiling.

As Don stretched to look over the ledge, a flurry of black bumped at his light and face. Screaming he jumped down and rolled in the dirt. Bats screeched as they dipped and lunged on their way out of the cave. Once everyone recovered from the scare, Don climbed back up.

About eighteen inches below the ceiling, Don felt a groove. The rock was not loose, but it had some unusual variations. He dug at the gap between the rocks with his hunting knife and loosened the first rock. The top eighteen inches had been walled in and covered with dirt to match the cave wall. Don let out a whoop!

When Don climbed down, he detailed his discovery.

Ray looked at his watch; they were almost due back home. "We better get out of here and come back with some tools and a ladder!"

They had dinner at the boys' house and could hardly wait to get back in the cave. The short ladder they located in the barn was perfect to drag through the narrow breakdown. As they gathered supplies, they found a rock hammer with a little pick on the back side and a camp shovel.

Ben came to the shed, and the boys greeted him excitedly. When he asked what all the gear was for, he was met with silence. The boys had learned long ago not to lie to their mom or dad, but they did not want to reveal their secret.

"It looks like you have been in the cave," Ben said. "Are you digging for treasure?"

Ray decided to go with his dad's suggestion. "Yes, sir. We decided to find lost gold in the cave."

"When I was your age, I searched the cave like everyone else. I did my fair share of digging." Sensing a teaching moment, Ben continued, "Let's say you find some coins or gold. It could change your lives. What would you do if you had a million dollars?"

Amber thought of the jars of cash in the cellar. She already had more cash than most people would ever have at one time. "I think I would see how much good I could do."

"How about you, Ray? What would you do with a million dollars?"

"I don't really know," he said. "For starters, I would get a dirt bike. Maybe I would save the rest."

Don said, "I would pay the taxes on it and invest half in annuities and half in real estate. I don't know what annuities are, but the man on the radio says that every week!"

Ben chuckled. "Here are some things to consider. If, as the legends go, there is Civil War gold in the cave, people would try to claim it. The United States government would want to claim it since they won the war. If there is gold, it is legal to own, but people will always try to get it for themselves. There are also greedy people like the ones who burned down the cabin back in 1900. They burned it to see if any gold was in the walls. Gold makes people do things they would not normally do. Maybe it is not the gold. Maybe it is greed or the fever. I can see the three of you already have a case of gold fever!

"Anyway, my advice is to have fun. Take the time to enjoy being kids. It's good to plan and dream, but when it comes to gold, keep your lips zipped. Every time the rumors start back, there is trouble. Riff-raff arrives, acting like they have the right to trespass. Amber, I am not talking about you. As far as I am concerned, you are the closest family Preston has. I know he can't wait to see you. It's late today. Wait until later to go in the cave. Spend the evening here with family. Amber, stay and join us for some games. If there is something in the cave, it's been there for a hundred years. A few more days won't matter."

Amber's diary entry: "Can adventure and friendship make pain go away?"

Amber went to sleep dreaming happily of friends and treasure hunting. Somewhere in the darkest hours, the nightmare of her ... little brother left her sobbing in tangled sheets.

*   *   *

The next day long letters were delivered to the farms. Preston was excited to hear Amber was in town and doing well. He had been very worried about her after the fire. He had been considering selling the farm even though it had been in the family for more than a century. Preston was 100 percent behind Britney's plan and included the signed papers for school.

The big news was that he and his new wife, Sheila, were building a home on a vast ranch she owned in Melbourne, Australia. The bigger news was they were coming back to visit the United States and stop in to see Amber.

6

Sheila and Preston watched the foundation being poured on the ranch house in Melbourne. By the time they returned from their six-week honeymoon, the house would be well underway. Though Sheila had traveled the world, she had not been to the great national parks of the United States. They modified their plans to stop first to check on the farm and his granddaughter, Amber, in Tennessee.

Preston was thrilled to have her on the farm, but he was uncertain whether she could manage on her own at only fourteen. Having Britney and Ben helping was reassuring. He had not seen Amber in two years. At twelve, she was tall and very smart. If the farm was still active with cattle, chickens, and goats, he would not have considered Britney's proposal.

He and Sheila had all the money they needed. Though he was a farmer, he had saved all his life. Sheila had sold her veterinary practice and done very well for herself. They had the five thousand-acre ranch in Melbourne and the new house all free and clear. Preston had considered selling the 260-acre farm. With his son no longer living and Lisa likely dead, he hatched a plan to keep the farm in the family. He had spent much of the previous week with lawyers and developed a plan to immediately gift the farm to Amber.

*   *   *

A week ahead of the original schedule, Preston's plane touched down in Nashville. After a trip down to the farm, they planned to drive over to Gatlinburg in the Great Smoky Mountains and start their national park honeymoon.

Preston and Sheila arrived in style in a red Cadillac. He still had a gate key and drove straight the house. He noticed the very large rock by the driveway and wondered when it was put there. It made sense. What good is a gate one could drive around? To his surprise, the yard was mowed—and new flowers were planted all around the front of the house. He honked the horn politely, and they got out of the car.

Amber looked up from cooking lunch and saw Preston and a ruggedly beautiful lady at his side. She ran down the steps and wrapped him in a big hug. After a moment, she composed herself and gave Sheila a big hug. Amber took off running toward the house and yelled, "Come on in!"

As Preston and Sheila approached the house, they smelled fried chicken.

When Amber came to the door, she was wearing an apron with the bold print "Grillin' Granddad." Preston recognized it as the apron he received last Christmas from Amber. "What's cooking?" asked Sheila. "It smells great!"

"I ran inside because the chicken was frying, and I didn't want it to burn."

The cookbook was open on the counter by the stove, and flour was scattered about. Overall, the kitchen was in good shape.

"What else are you having?"

"Maybe we will have something from a can. Do you like beans or peaches? I haven't learned to cook more than one thing at a time yet."

As they ate, Amber asked all about Sheila and Australia. The stories came easily. Sheila was the woman Amber wanted to be: smart, outspoken, and capable of almost anything. She had traveled the world and done extraordinary things.

Preston said how very sorry he was about the fire and the horrible toll on her family. He asked about Amber's mom. Amber had been curious but afraid to ask the authorities about her mother because it might get her in trouble with Child Protective Services. Preston agreed to try to locate Lisa and check on her condition.

Amber told Preston and Sheila about her adventures with Ray and Don.

Sheila loved the campfire story. Amber's antics brought memories of her own youthful misadventures. An owl hooted. To Preston and Sheila's surprise, Amber put her fists to her lips and returned a hoot.

A few minutes later, Ray and Don appeared at the door.

Amber said, "Grab a plate and come on in. You need to meet somebody." Introductions were made with polite handshakes.

Sheila asked if they had been camping lately, and they all laughed.

Amber considered telling Preston about the scruffy characters who tried to steal the riding mower, but she decided not to concern him. She thanked Preston for helping with the paperwork to get her into school. With school matters settled, she could concentrate on the adventures in the cave.

Preston said he was going next door to talk with Britney and Ben, and he left Sheila to get to know the kids a little better.

* * *

With a satchel of papers in hand, Preston knocked at the door. He greeted Britney with a hug and Ben with a sturdy handshake.

"You are about a week ahead of schedule, aren't you?" asked Britney.

"Yes, I wanted to pop in unannounced and get a feel for how Amber managed the farm. It looks great. Amber has grown a foot in the past two years and is quite the young lady. Those boys of yours are growing too. They are fine young men. You should be very proud."

"We are," replied Britney. "We have been keeping a close eye on the three of them. Both boys have had a crush on Amber since they spent the summer together two years ago."

Preston's eyes sparkled, and he said, "So tell me, are they behaving themselves?"

"Neither would likely admit it, but it seems they have grown very close in the past few weeks. They are more like brothers and sister, really best friends."

Preston nodded his approval and said, "Well, I came to talk some business. I considered selling the farm and giving Amber a substantial part of the money. She is my only relative I know to be living. I got a letter from Amber's mom, Lisa, about the time she left for Mexico. In addition to the fire and her husband being charged with arson, she has late-stage cancer. Apparently, she left to get experimental treatment in Mexico. There is a good chance she is dead by now. Amber does not know. Lisa couldn't bear to tell her at the time. I have not heard from her since she left. Maybe I can get someone down there to find her. Meanwhile, I have written a new will. It is official and notarized.

"What I am doing is unusual. I am working out a plan to go ahead and give the farm to Amber now. If I should croak before it all gets finalized, it is left to her in the will. In the next few days, when I get this all set, it will belong to her—even though she is a minor. I will be her custodian, but I will be in Australia. I need someone here to act as a guardian to help with decisions and to put an adult's rational mind to things. I am not asking you to cosign any notes, but to go to bat for her if someone starts taking advantage of her as a kid. You won't have any legal liabilities. I'm going to pay the taxes for the next seven years. I think the county will accept the money early."

"Are you sure this is all legal?" asked Britney.

"It took some doing, but it's supposed to be airtight. I am going to talk with the sheriff, the judge, and the clinic to let them know what is going on so they can be supportive. They have always treated me well, and I expect they will treat Amber the same."

*   *   *

Preston and Sheila stayed for another two days, visiting and doing business in town. Preston asked the Spark family over for dinner. After a scrumptious meal prepared by Amber and Sheila, everyone had strawberry shortcake.

While Sheila brought out coffee, Preston retrieved his satchel of papers. He said, "While everyone is here, I have an announcement to make. As you know, Sheila and I will be going back to Australia after we spend several more weeks traveling in the US. This old farm has been in the Preston family for more than a hundred years. People have been badgering me for the past few years to sell the place. Some have become downright insistent. Pushy people rub me the wrong way. I have recently changed my will and designated Amber to receive the farm when I die."

Everyone looked at Amber for reaction.

She was stunned.

Preston said, "However, I have changed my mind. I am giving the farm to her now. In the event the folks I have looking for Lisa locate her, I have made some provisions for her as well. Amber, what do you say? Are you ready to be a landowner?"

The table erupted with congratulations.

Amber was without words. She never expected anything like this. The boys slapped her on the back, and Preston slid papers over for her to sign. Ben and Britney signed some forms and witnessed Amber's documents. Preston packed his satchel, left copies for Amber, and told her there was a bank account in her name with a little money in it to get started.

Amber walked over to Preston, thanked him, hugged him, and cried for a long time. When she regained her composure, she wisely turned to everyone at the table, thanked them all, and told them she would be asking for their help in the coming days.

7

Bordertown Clinic, Tijuana, Mexico

Lisa Preston Butler looked awful by any standards. Her hollow eyes and pale complexion were like many in the border town clinic. Most were beyond treatment in the US and spending whatever they had to prolong death. There were days when Lisa wished she had stayed at home and died. The chemo and radiation were torture.

She had no appetite, and her treatments rendered food tasteless. Every few days, another empty room appeared on the hall. A skeletal ghost stared back in her mirror, taunting her to join the others.

Looking away from the mirror, she took pleasure in the nearby mountains. She longed to hike and swim again. Setting a lofty goal to hike to the top of that mountain someday, she shared her dream with her Physician Assistant who was head of nursing.

He approached her with a smile. "You look better today. Your test results are favorable. May I get anything for you?"

Lisa said, "When I get better, get me some hiking boots and a guide to take me to the top of that mountain."

He said, "Get better—and I will guide you. I have been there many times. You will love it. Today I have new medicine for you." Before she could complain, he rolled in a cart with her food and a bouquet of roses. "This is all the medicine you get today," he said.

8

After Preston and Sheila got on their way to the Great Smoky Mountains, Amber, Ray, and Don were finally able to go back to the cave. The excitement of the past few days had still not sunk in. Amber owned the land, the house, the equipment, and the cave!

Amber lifted the end of the ladder over the rocks as they dragged their equipment into the cave. When they passed the round room, they found what they suspected was a small passage near the roof that had been sealed for more than a hundred years. With the ladder in place, they did rock paper scissors to see who got to dig out the rocks and have the first look. Don won with rocks over their scissors. Amber held the ladder steady while Ray passed the tools. Everyone stood back to make room for the rocks and dirt Don was tearing away from the makeshift wall.

"What are you seeing?" asked Amber. With her Instamatic flash camera, she took Don's picture when he turned around. She passed him the camera, and he took pictures of the hole he was making and of Ray and Amber in the cave.

Although Amber wanted to document the discovery, she was not sure how to get the pictures developed without someone figuring out they had found the treasure. Don soon tired out, and Ray climbed the ladder.

When the rocks were removed from the first part of the tunnel, it revealed a mostly round channel in solid rock. The passage was barely large enough to crawl in with smooth rock all around. No one knew how deep they would have to dig.

Ray told Don and Amber to step back to one side while he pitched rocks into the cave. Soon, he was standing on the top rung and waist-deep in the hole. The passage seemed to be a smooth wormhole through solid rock. About three feet in, broken pieces of rock remained wedged loosely overhead. After the debris in the passage was cleared, no end was in sight.

Amber took a turn next. After ten minutes, she stopped. "I found a bottle." She dug a few more seconds and revealed a clear whiskey bottle with a cork in place. Inside was a rolled piece of paper. She photographed the bottle with the note inside as Ray extracted the paper with a twist of his knife.

Amber said, "The note was dated 'In the year of our Lord 1934.'"

"Meaning what?" asked Ray.

"It means 1934," replied Don with a grin.

Amber said, "I thought we were looking for gold left here in 1865. Maybe the note solves the mystery."

> If you found this note, you're probably looking for the
> lost payroll shipment. My wife, Nellie, spent six years
> searching for treasure. It might be best to put the rocks

back and forget you came this far. I have seen people die of yellow fever, but I think gold fever is worse. People go crazy when they get the scent of gold. It cost me my wife—and any hope of having a family. If you keep going, God be with you. Don't let the desire for riches or fame take root where love and joy should grow.

In the year of our Lord 1934,

Nat Preston III

Amber said, "Maybe we should think through what to do next."

Ray said, "For one thing, we need to plan for all these rocks we are throwing down."

"No, I mean, should we keep digging?"

"We have to," said Don. "We can't stop now. Remember what Dad asked. What would we do if we found it? How can we protect it? Anyone could come and take it."

Amber said, "Let's dig some more. When we see what's there, we can decide."

Don climbed the ladder, dug for a few minutes, and stopped. "I broke through. It's a room." He had been passing rocks back along his body and dropping them near the ladder. He noticed some small rocks kept dropping on his legs from the top of the passage.

"Can you see anything?" Ray was on the ladder and looking behind Don.

"It's too dark! It's a big room."

"Push more rocks into the room so you can see."

Amber passed up a brighter flashlight. "Try this one."

A slow whistle came from the passage. As Don shined the light, he whispered. "This is not good!" Though his view was limited, Don could see what looked like a few mummified bodies in rotted uniforms. A different smell was coming from this room. He was not surprised with what was lying around. It looked like the floor of the room was about ten feet below. Don scrambled out of the passage and cleared out the last of the debris.

Ray went in next. On one side of the room, there was a small wooden box with steel straps and handles. The glimmer of gold caught his eye. It looked like coins. He backed out, and Amber took a turn. Seeing what looked like bodies made her think of her own close brush with death and the injuries in the fire. Reflections of bits of gold in the dust brought her back to present.

Amber huddled with Ray and Don near the ladder. She said, "This is a grave or a crypt. Soldiers appear to have died in here. There are probably laws about desecrating a grave site."

Don said, "We know where it is; we can't leave it here. Someone else can come in here, see all these rocks, and figure it out. Besides, we aren't desecrating—we are exploring. And even if we find more gold, we won't bother the bodies."

Amber said, "If we decide to go in, we don't have a ladder on the inside to climb down."

Ray said, "I think I should go in and check this out. I'll climb down a knotted rope tied to the ladder. You two hold the ladder."

Amber said, "Tie a second rope to the ladder and take it along. When you find something to bring out, tie it to the rope or put it in your pack, and we can pull it up and out."

Don said, "Good idea. Now let's have some water and a candy bar and get started."

Amber was already getting food out of the pack.

Ray turned at the top of the ladder and put his feet in first. He climbed backward until he was near the edge. His feet were dangling over into the crypt. With the toe of his boot, he felt a small ledge.

Holding tightly to the rope, Ray bounced some weight on the unseen ledge. It felt secure—and then it snapped off beneath his foot. He dropped. The rope jerked the ladder off the floor. Ray's light could not illuminate his feet, but he continued to let himself down the rope by feeling his way along. Once on solid ground, he released the rope and looked around.

The four bodies wore Confederate uniforms. There were even bandages on them. There did not appear to be any skeletons. The tattered uniforms were propped in a sitting position, but there were no bodies! Scattered on the floor were some playing cards, a Bible, a tiny notebook, and some gold coins. Ray pocketed a few flawless twenty-dollar gold pieces.

Amber called out, "You okay in there?"

"I'm fine. It doesn't seem right to talk loud even though there don't seem to be any bodies in the uniforms."

Ray went to the first of five small steel strongboxes. The top creaked on its rusty hinges. A glow seemed to come from in the box as he moved his flashlight across the contents. Candy bar-sized gold bars were stacked nearly to the top. Large gold coins topped the bars like icing on a cake. A few bars were missing from the top row, but when he lifted a bar, he was unprepared for the weight and almost dropped it. It was as heavy as lead. The bar weighed a few pounds, and its smooth molded surface was marked with symbols.

He put one in each front pocket, one in the back, and ten more in his pack. He tied it to the rope and went back over to the soldiers. He gathered a notebook, a Bible, and a small lapel pin from the dirt floor. He put them in the pack and called for Amber to pull the rope.

"Stop it at the top," he said. "You can climb up to the passage and lower it down. The pack is heavier than it looks."

Ray examined the wall below the passage. Footholds had been

carved into the stone, making a crude set of steps toward the opening. Using them and the rope, he went quickly to the top. A bit more debris had fallen near the center of the passage, delaying his return.

They spent an hour scattering the rocks all along the edge of the main cave—so they looked more natural and did not point to the newly discovered opening. Once the ladder was moved, the high passage was hardly noticeable. They left the cave with all their gear and the ladder.

Ray's pack was heavy, but he did not seem to mind. Back at the Preston farmhouse, Amber insisted on a picture before they cleaned up.

During the meal of sandwiches, Ray reached into a pocket and pulled out three gold coins and one larger yellow brass coin. From his other pockets he pulled out three shiny bars of gold. Tipping the pack, he poured out the Bible, the notebook, the lapel pin, and ten more gleaming gold bars.

Mesmerized by the gold, no one spoke.

The gold pieces were unbelievable heavy and hard to pick up, but they were even more difficult to put down. Amber retrieved a bathroom scale, and the pile of thirteen bars weighed more than twenty-six pounds.

Don had been doing some research and figured gold was worth about $1,700 per pound. Doing the math in his head, he estimated the gold on the scale was worth about $44,000.

"And there are five boxes down there," said Ray.

"How many bars do you think are in each box?" asked Don.

"I think there were about ten bars in each row—and they could have been five rows deep."

Don quickly did the math. "About five hundred pounds would be about $850,000!"

Amber said, "I wonder if it is worth more as artifacts of the Civil War? Let's pack the gold away and hide it."

They each got a bar and a coin to hide for themselves. The main bundle of ten bars was wrapped in paper and put in a shoebox in the attic. It was not marked or made to stand out among the other boxes. They took a final look and returned to the table.

Ray asked for the extra yellow brass colored coin for an idea he had.

Because it was Amber's property, Don said it was her decision.

Amber smiled and put her arms around the boys. "You are right. It is my property, but we found the treasure. We are in this together. One for all, and all for one. Ray, you are welcome to the extra coin. Remember what your dad said? 'Keep your lips zipped.' I am so proud to have you two as friends. We make quite a team. I think we need a name for ourselves. Try to think of a cool name. We can compare ideas later."

Ray pocketed the extra coin, and they turned their attention to the Bible. It had an inscription in the front: "Presented to my dear son George Smith, January 3, 1861, by Geneva Smith. Fight well and Godspeed." There was also a short account of how they came to be in the cave.

They turned their attention to the notebook, and Amber opened it. The soldier's name was in the front. The writing was as difficult to read as the original note she received from her mother.

Entries were often made weeks apart, starting in the spring of 1863, and the tiny script was mostly about missing home and hating the carnage of battle. At only sixteen years old, the author had joined the Confederate Army. He had seen soldiers younger than himself die in battle. Close fighting using bayonets was the worst. He described the battlefield, when the smoke cleared, as "a writhing hell."

Amber stopped reading at the memory of her own smoking hell. She closed her eyes, and in the silence, she smelled the stench—for a moment she was back there screaming his name. When she looked up, the boys had tears in their eyes too. They had never asked Amber about her injuries from the fire. She sensed their discomfort and decided it was time to explain. She rolled up one of her sleeves to her shoulder. The skin at the top of her arm was pink and scarred. "We have gone weeks and neither of you have asked me about the night of the fire or about my injuries. I appreciate you accepting me without asking questions. I never intend for anyone to see the extent of my scarring. I will tell you it's like this." She held out her arm. "I will always wear shirts to cover me from the waist up. Needless to say, you don't want to see me in a bikini."

Don and Ray were surprised by her candor.

Ray said, "However you look, I think you're great."

Don said, "I do too. Who cares if you keep your shirt on?"

They first smiled, and then all laughed uncontrollably as they realized the absurdity of what Don had said.

Amber knew, in that moment, that she had true friends for the first time in her life. She made a silent vow to always be true to them.

Amber's diary entry: "I need to trust myself enough to trust others. Stay true to friends. This time don't let bad things happen."

9

The dire warning on the note in the bottle bothered Amber. Something bad must have happened to Nat and his wife. He was obviously the one who filled in the passage. She made a mental note to talk with Preston and find out more about the family history. She wondered if Nat Preston III ever had kids.

Meanwhile, it was time to make another trip to the crypt. This time, they traveled lighter and planned to bring back more gold. The plan was to lift out fifteen bars at a time, and when a strongbox was empty, they would take out the box.

Amber went first, bringing both ropes. One had been knotted to make it easier to climb. The other was tied to a sturdy pack to hold the gold bars. Ray had explained the footholds. Amber brought in a battery-powered lantern to light the room. Clearing the debris and small rocks from the center of the tunnel slowed her progress. She took a few pictures to document the room. Looking all around the room, she noticed a small passage similar to the one they had already cleared. It was on the opposite side of the room and close to the ceiling.

She loaded the pack with fifteen gold bars. Don had cleverly tied the pack in the middle of the long rope this time. After Ray and Don hauled the pack up and through the tunnel, Amber let it down slowly on the other side. Then she pulled the empty pack back for more. This worked great for seven loads. While the pack was pulling through with the eighth load of gold bars, it stopped midway in the little tunnel. Alternately pulling it back and forth, Ray finally got it to pull through. Rock debris came down with the pack. Then there was a scraping sound, and dust billowed from the tiny tunnel.

Don nearly leaped to the top of the ladder. Shining the light inside, he could see a slab of rock almost completely blocking the tunnel. It had crushed down sealing the passage. He could tell it extended into the rock above like a sliding door. Amber was trapped!

Pinpoints of light came around the rock through the dust. Don called to Amber. "Are you okay?"

"Yes. What happened?"

"The tunnel caved in."

Amber pulled herself easily up the rope toward the tunnel. It was blocked solid. From where she stood, the solid rock looked like a gravestone. The words in the bottle came back to her. "It cost me my wife." For a second, she could visualize her epitaph on the stone. What would it read?

Here lies Amber, who took foolish risks.

Here lies Amber, fearless explorer who went where no man has ever gone.

Don's shout broke into her reverie, and she said, "Can you hear me, Don?"

"Yes, I can barely hear you. This one rock is blocking everything. It must be eighteen inches thick."

"Get Ray on the ladder too. We need help, but we have some time. There is a small cavity not much farther back in the cave. Take the box and gold there and cover them with the rocks. Then get a piece of pipe in the barn and a hammer. I have the lantern and a flashlight. Before this is over, I might need some food and water. We can drive the pipe in beside the rock where the light comes through. Maybe some air can come through too. Now please move the gold and get your mom and dad. They will know what to do next."

Amber used the time to look around. She moved a soldier's uniform around and found a letter addressed to his wife. It started with "we are trapped." She wondered if she would remain trapped. She thought back on what she had been through in the past year. Nothing could be worse than the pain of the burns. For days, she was slathered in salves while floating on a layer of air on a special bed. The drugs only dulled the constant pain. Then they had to debride the burns. Every few days, they peeled away scabs and thick membranes so the burns could heal from the inside out. It was awful but necessary, according to the nurses. The burns finally healed completely. It was not pretty, but the pain was minimal. She had poured her soul into rehab. The pain of working out and stretching the new skin and tissue was nothing compared to the first few weeks after the fire. As if the scars were not enough, the vivid memory of the fire, the smoke, and the smells came back often. And then there was guilt—darker than the smoke—worse than the acrid smells. Shaking her head to clear the thoughts, she focused on her dilemma.

Motivated to make the best of her situation, she shined her light around and looked for any available resources. In the corner, there was a stack of four rusty rifles. She wondered if they would still shoot. She momentarily wondered, *if things get bad enough, will I find out?*

There was a long sword and a bayonet. She picked one old rifle and looked it over carefully. It had a little brass door on the stock and some white lead balls inside. In the stock was a cavity deep in the wood with some kind of pungent grease inside.

She gathered all the gold coins she could find and piled them in one of the strongboxes. Many of them were covered in dust. Tiring of this, she decided to see if she could climb to the other small tunnel she had seen before.

She used the bayonet to clear away the dirt and improve her footholds. She worked her way to the top and over to the opening. The passage was almost identical in size to the one they had cleared, but it was open. Moving with caution and vowing to be extra careful, she inched her way into the tunnel with her little flashlight in front of her. It was an easy crawl, but the passage began to narrow. Amber was keenly aware it was too small to turn around. As the tunnel narrowed, she came to something in the passage. It looked like half-rotted leather. Retrieving it, she realized it was the dried remains of skin and bones. The bones had huge claws.

Amber's scream in the tunnel was deafening. She could hear the muted calls of Don and Ray far behind her. After calming down and regaining her composure, she moved forward. This was no soldier. It was the skeletal remains of a large animal. From the size of the claws, it was a bear. Amber choked back revulsion as she attempted to crawl through the bones. It was impossible. The passage was narrower than before. There was a tipped-over kerosene lantern ahead of her. She grabbed the skull and some other large bones and backed out until the passage was larger. Depositing the bones along the side of the passage, she moved back toward the skeleton. She retrieved the lantern and some more large bones before backing out again and depositing the bones along the side again. Amber hoped the bear did not catch whoever had the lantern before getting stuck in the cave. It made her think about the note: "It cost me my wife and family."

Amber backed out one last time and carried the huge bear skull back down to the floor of the cave. She noticed her lantern was dimmer than before. She turned it off and used her flashlight to climb the rope. She was careful to keep most of her weight on the footholds in case the rope had been damaged by the slab of rock that was blocking her passage.

Don was back on the ladder. "What happened in there?"

"I found another small passage and followed it for a while. There was a skeleton of a bear in the passage, which I was not expecting."

"Can you get out?"

"I don't know. The bear didn't, but it was bigger. My batteries are getting low too."

"Ray went to find Dad. I'm sure they will bring help."

"I am sure he will. I will need water soon. If you could get a pipe in here, you could pour water through it."

"I don't want to leave you here alone."

"Go ahead and try to get a pipe, some water, and a funnel. I'm not alone."

Don could not see her, but he knew she was smiling. "Okay. Don't go away," he said. "I will be back soon."

"Bring some AA batteries. Maybe they will fit through the pipe."

* * *

Ray went to get his dad, but he was not home. He told his mom, and she got on the phone to try to locate him. She wanted to know the specifics and how she could help.

Ray put some tools in the car and asked his mom to call the sheriff. As they drove over to the Preston farm, he explained how the rock was blocking the passage.

Don was heading out to find the pipe and batteries when he met Ray going in with a hammer and the other supplies.

Britney went back to Preston's house and made a few follow-up calls. She had an itinerary for Preston and Sheila and a phone number for the hotel where he would be if he was on schedule.

10

Word traveled fast in a small town, and the rescue squad arrived just before the looky-loos. The sheriff had everyone except the rescue squad stay away from the cave, including the reporter. It was as if people had been asked to come over for a picnic. They sat on the porch and parked in the yard. Fortunately, no one was bold enough to go in the house. A realtor with slicked-back hair, who had been eyeing the property for years, took the opportunity to look around, peek in windows, and generally be nosy. He tried to get access to the cave, but the sheriff turned him away.

* * *

Before the rescue squad got to the scene, Don climbed the ladder with the pipe and drove it beside the rock along the edge of the wall. He pushed six AA batteries into the pipe, followed them with a wire, and pushed them out. When Amber was ready at the other end, he poured water into the funnel.

Amber drank as fast as she could. She put a finger over the pipe and rested. "Enough, thanks."

The rescue squad took over and got all the details from Ray and Don. They admitted they were treasure hunting but made no mention of what they found. The focus stayed on rescuing Amber.

The rescue squad brought their own ladder and soon had a man assessing the problem. The Jaws of Life were put into the cracks below the rock. Even with all the hydraulic force they could generate, the rock did not budge. The lead rescuer complimented Don on the pipe idea, and he gave all the credit to Amber.

"The girl is smart," said the rescuer.

The next plan was to break the rock and pull out the pieces. However, they figured more would fall back down. In order to cut through the rock, they sent for an air-powered drill. Hoses had to be run from a compressor outside the cave.

Three hours passed, and the drill was still not running. They had to get operators who were familiar with the machines. They were going to try to jackhammer one side of the rock, set a steel block under the rock, and remove the other side. As a backup, another crew was planning to jackhammer a new tunnel at floor level straight through the eight or ten feet of rock. No one knew how long that would take.

Amber was impatient. She crawled back into the skeleton tunnel with her flashlight, extra batteries, and a length of rope she had cut with the bayonet. Whispering a little prayer, she crawled over the remainder of the bear skeleton.

The passage angled slightly down, and Amber was conscious of how difficult it would be to back out. There was a bend to the left and a spot that was wide enough to sit and turn around if needed. That was a miracle. Her scar tissue from the burns was scratched and scraped from crawling on her stomach. She wondered how the rescue people were doing. She had a feeling there were problems and decided to do what she could while she had energy and batteries.

11

The rescue squad was having trouble. Once the air drill was in place, they hammered away at the huge rock. A fracture unexpectedly appeared in the rock. By the time they saw the diagonal fracture, it was too late. The huge rock shifted along the fracture and wedged itself even more tightly in the passage. When smoke from friction and dust from drilling cleared, they saw the crushed pipe. Not a sliver of light came around the boulder. More debris from above threatened to come down around the rock.

In another passage, a hundred feet away, Amber put a new set of batteries in her little flashlight and pocketed the old ones. The light was even dimmer with the replacement batteries. She decided to use them before changing batteries again. She was able to crawl forward on all fours. She moved quickly, light wagged back and forth as her hand took each step.

The passage split, but without a compass, Amber had no idea which direction she was headed. She went right. The passage got larger and opened into a room. Unlike the path she had been walking, the floor of the room had huge cracks. Looking inside a crack, she saw the edge of a smooth surface. It felt like pottery. Carefully reaching inside and pulling it free, she retrieved a small bottle. With her light dimming, she slipped the bottle into her pocket.

The ceiling was fifty feet overhead. She was in what looked like a well that was about ten feet in diameter. The walls were worn smooth by thousands of years of water flow and the mild acid in the water. Her light went out, but Amber shook the flashlight and a dim light returned. On a whim, she used a battery to write her name, the date, and a short message in the soft dirt.

She changed to another set of batteries, but they were not much better. Reversing course, she hurried back to the fork in the passage. This time, she took the other fork. The passage angled down more and curved to the right. The batteries grew weaker, and she only had one nearly drained set remaining. She considered going back. If her batteries failed, she would have to crawl back in the dark. She continued forward.

Hearing something ahead, she stopped. There were small pieces of driftwood along the passage. The sound of water gently moving through rocks broke the silence. The air here was different. It had a slightly pungent odor. It smelled like the river! Amber eased around a bend. More sticks lined the floor. Old weathered driftwood was scattered everywhere. The floor sloped gently toward a distant wall, and there was water! As she reached the edge of the pool, she could see the passage ended in water and a solid rock face. Her light grew dimmer and went out.

Amber stood in wonder. As her night vision improved in the darkness, a shape came into sight. It was pale and gray at first, but then it became more defined. Faint light was coming from beneath the wall at the end of the pool. It was dim but definitely light. In the water, about four feet under the wall, absolute darkness gave way to a lighter shade of gray.

Amber was a good swimmer, but she had never tried anything like this. She considered using her last batteries but decided swimming to the light of the river might be smarter. She walked down the slope until the water was to her waist. She tied the rope to a cracked rock near the edge of the water. Holding the rope, she let it out as she got deeper and deeper. Taking a final look into the water, she pocketed her flashlight, held her breath, ducked under, and gazed in the direction of the river. After coming back up for air, she ducked under again and swam hard toward the light, paying out rope as she swam. Suddenly, she hit something. As she was about through the tunnel, something seemed to grab her in the dark. Whatever it was, would not release her. Her boot slipped through an opening in the wire and trapped her foot. The harder she pulled, the tighter it pulled against her ankle.

With air running out, she told herself not to panic. Reaching for her boot laces in the dark, she clawed at whatever she could feel—one string and then another. The boot stripped off of her foot. Her vision was getting black around the edges, and her ears were ringing. There was not much time left. She still had the rope in her hand and began to pull frantically. She saw only black, but she could still feel the rope. Amber pulled and pulled for her life. Finally feeling the bottom, she stood, gasped for air, and screamed in frustration. Seeing nothing in the blackness, she was glad she had the rope as her guide. For the moment, air was enough. Then standing shoulder deep in the icy water, she began to shiver violently head to toe.

In the dark, Amber took out her flashlight and struggled to turn it on. She confirmed the weak beam still worked underwater. Taking another deep breath, she ducked back under the rock. This time, with the flashlight pointing ahead, she could see the wires dangling over half the opening. She veered to the right, and as she cleared the fence, she let the rope fall away. Skirting the rock ledge above, and guided by the increasing light, Amber swam hard for the surface. She launched high out of the water and took in a welcomed breath. The daylight and the fresh air were amazing.

Amber crawled onto the riverbank at the base of the bluff and lay on her back for a moment staring into the blue sky. She marked the exact spot where the cave opened into the river. It took her another ten minutes to make her way along the steep riverbank with only one boot. When she rounded the corner of the bluff, she was surprised to see cars, trucks, and a big diesel machine. She walked behind some people and asked what was going on. Several wild stories were circulating already. No one even recognized her. Amber saw a small crowd of people—and the sheriff—near the cave entrance. She straightened her wet clothes as much as possible and approached the sheriff, walking with as much dignity as possible with only one sloshing boot.

"Hello, sir. I think you've been looking for me. I am Amber Preston."

A camera flashed as she shook the sheriff's hand.

The local reporter had the scoop. Shoving a microphone in her face, the reporter started asking questions.

Amber said, "I need to get in there and find my friends."

12

Amber made her way to the cave. Near the entrance, Britney wrapped her in a tight embrace. After assuring Britney she was okay, she started toward the cave.

"Wait," Britney called out. She took off her shoe and held it out for Amber to step into. She laced it while sitting on the ground. Neither noticed the camera flash.

With a thank you, Amber ducked into the cave with the sheriff's flashlight. There were some temporary lights in the cave and lots of noise. She passed the entrance to the round room and approached the rescue workers. Shouts rang out over the equipment as Ray and Don saw her coming. All three hugged tightly for a minute and then felt awkward as the equipment went silent and everyone stared.

The chief of the rescue squad smiled and said, "Amber, I presume? Are you okay?"

"Hungry, wet, and tired, but I'm glad to be free. I took a chance, crawled through a tiny passage, and eventually got out."

"You need to see our medic to be checked. You may be hypothermic. We need to get you into some dry clothes and wrapped in a blanket."

"First let me see where you were drilling." She climbed the ladder. The rock had been drilled apart, but it had fallen back down and sealed the passage even tighter. She saw the pipe crushed and flattened into the rock wall.

Amber said, "I appreciate all you have done to try to rescue me. Sorry for causing so much trouble. Thankfully we can all go home now."

A rescuer draped blankets over her shoulders and she pulled them tight around her wet clothes.

As men packed their gear, one rescuer wandered around shining his light further back in the cave. His supervisor called out to him with orders to help haul the equipment out.

Amber walked up to the main rescue worker and said, "Do you have a sign we can post to warn people not to come in the cave? It is private property, but you know how some people will want to come take a look for themselves."

"Young lady, we have just the thing."

Once outside, the paramedics offered to examine Amber and transport her to the hospital.

She thanked them but declined.

The rescue chief showed her the signs which read: "Keep Out, Private Property, Written Permission of Owner Required for Access." There was a blank space at the bottom for a signature. After handing a permanent marker to Amber for her signature, the sheriff signed his name and the word sheriff on each one. He handed them to a deputy with instructions to put them near the entrance.

Standing nearby, the nosy realtor fumed with resentment.

The sheriff gave Amber a knowing wink and said, "Now get home and get warm. I will come by tomorrow to talk."

As she and the Sharp family walked to the porch, a camera flash blinded Amber for a moment. The reporter was front and center with a microphone and more questions. "How did you get out? Why were you so wet? Did the rescue team open the passage? Were you really trapped? Some people are saying this is a stunt."

Ben stepped forward and said, "Tammy, Amber needs to get a shower, eat, and get warm. If you come back tomorrow at noon, we can have a talk. No more questions tonight."

In a long, hot shower, Amber felt the scarring burn from the numerous scrapes and cuts. In a way, it felt good. The pain reminded her she was alive—not only alive but living—and she was living an exciting life with good friends. She began to cry at the thought of all she had been through. The tears turned to tears of joy when her thoughts came back to the present. She was so thankful for her good friends.

13

Amber got up early the next morning, ate a quick breakfast, and pulled the small bottle from her jeans as she prepared to wash her clothes. It was hardly a bottle at all. Misshapen and flat on one side, it was barely the size of a saltshaker. The top was sealed with a small ceramic plug and some glassy amber glue. After trying to scrape the sealant and remove the plug, she cracked the little bottle. Over a paper towel, she separated the pieces. There was nothing inside but five seeds and what looked like crushed shells. The seeds were wrinkled and looked like large brown raisins. She put three in a small jar in the pantry. Outside, where she had planted flowers by the house, she scratched two holes, planted and watered the seeds.

Expecting the sheriff, Amber left the front gate open. At ten o'clock, the familiar sound of tires on the gravel road announced his arrival. He waited respectfully by his car for Amber and Ben to come to the porch. Amber invited him to come into the kitchen, and they sat around the table.

After inquiring if Amber was feeling okay, the sheriff said, "Over the years, almost everyone in the county has been in Preston cave, and most were poking around looking for treasure. I made a few trips in there myself when I was younger. I'm afraid this incident is going to have this place crawling with treasure hunters and looky-loos. Preston came to see me before he took off for his honeymoon. He asked me to help keep an eye on you, and I'm glad to do it. When I was younger, your grandpa took me in and helped me when I was in a tight spot. I owe him a lot, and I don't forget a favor. Also, it is not wise—and it's sometimes illegal—to make false statements to an officer. So, if I ask you something, and you can't answer honestly, or don't want to answer for some reason, don't speak. Understand?"

She smiled.

He nodded and said, "The way you three have been grinning since the rescue, I suspect you found something. Whether you have or not, you could be in danger. People get gold fever and act like fools. Some will do almost anything to get their hands on a treasure. Now here's the deal. Say, hypothetically, you did find some amount of gold. It should be put in the bank for safekeeping. It would also be wise to let everyone know it is found so people will not keep looking. I know you don't know who to trust and may be ignorant of the laws about found treasure and so forth, but if a person had such a treasure, they should get a lawyer." He smiled and slid a card across the table. "This fellow is as honest as the day is long, which is rare for a lawyer. He knows about treasure. A few years ago, he was on a team of lawyers for some fellows who found a sunken riverboat on the Missouri. It had some payroll gold on board. A lawyer will need a retainer. It is a prepayment to engage services."

Amber said, "Preston told me to trust you. A few people let me down in the past year. Being around here with the Sharps and Preston,

I'm beginning to trust people again. Hypothetically, how much retainer would be required to secure the services of this lawyer?"

"Probably five hundred dollars. He is expensive."

"Would you happen to be seeing this lawyer anytime soon?"

"As a matter fact, he has an office in town. I'll pass it on the way to the jail."

Amber went to the bedroom and returned a few minutes later with five well-worn hundred-dollar bills. "I figure a girl in town by herself should have a lawyer on ... what was the term, retainer? Since we are speaking hypothetically, how could something valuable best be transported to a bank for safekeeping, especially if it were not cash?"

"If a person wanted to make sure people knew there was no more treasures to be found, one could hire an armored truck to make a delivery. It would get the attention of everyone and hopefully stop treasure hunters from coming around."

Amber's grin showed lots of teeth.

Ben was silently marveling at Amber's maturity. The day before, she had gone through a life-or-death struggle. Today, she was bantering with the sheriff like a pro.

At the sound of an approaching car, they expected to see the reporter. Amber, Ben, and the sheriff walked out on the porch to greet her. A long, shiny car that no one immediately recognized nosed in close to the house. A big man with slicked-back hair stepped out and looked around. "I'm looking for Preston." He offered his card to the sheriff. "Victor Deal ... I deal in real estate. I've had my eye on this place for a while, and I even made an offer on it a few years back. Would Preston be around?"

Amber said, "Preston is not in town, but I can assure you the property is not for sale."

Victor said, "I will check back when Preston is back in town. I am sure we can come to an agreement."

The sheriff said, "You have already been told by the owner, it is not for sale. Miss Preston is the owner. I think she spoke clearly. The property is not for sale."

Mr. Deal looked a little upset by the news—and he looked like one of the looky-loos trying to get in the cave the day before.

Another car lumbered down the driveway. Tammy and a photographer approached the house.

The sheriff said, "Come on in, Tammy. Mr. Deal was just leaving."

They made introductions, and Amber asked them to come inside and sit down. Tammy wanted to go to the cave and take some pictures. Amber insisted on keeping the interview short and around the kitchen table. Amber said, "The cave is off limits right now. Let's do an initial interview and if it goes well, we will schedule a series of articles."

Amber liked Tammy and hoped she could be trusted to be honest in what she reported. Amber said, "Why are you interested in this story?"

Tammy was caught off guard. She had planned to ask all the questions.

Amber waited.

Tammy said, "When I first heard you were trapped in the cave, my fear of going in there a few years ago came back. My plan was to write a sensational story about how scared you were and how the brave men rescued you. I realize now I wanted to write my story. It turns out you were nothing like me. You were courageous and concerned about your friends and how they felt. Your first act after escaping was to go to your friends and tell them you were okay. I want to write your story of friendship and bravery."

Amber asked, "Where do you want to begin?"

Before Tammy could answer, there was the sound of an owl in the distance.

Ray and Don walked to the porch, and Amber introduced them to

Tammy and the photographer. Amber explained how she was doing an interview with Tammy from the newspaper. "I want you two to sit in and be a part of the interview. Since she is a reporter, we will have to be careful about what we say. Let's get started."

Tammy said, "You are new in town. People only know what they read in the papers about the fire. If I write your story, people will know you. You will be starting school soon. I think a true story about you and your adventure can make your acceptance in this community go more smoothly."

Amber agreed to a series of interviews and told Tammy she would always be truthful with her. However, she would not always tell her everything. "Everyone does not need to know everyone's business. And some things only need to be known at the right time."

Tammy said, "You are smart, savvy, sharp, and not as naïve as most kids your age." Lifting a glass of iced tea, she said, "Here's to you, Amber, your good friends, and good stories to come."

Amber said, "Here's to lasting friendships and adventures."

They all clinked their tea glasses.

The sheriff decided to give a pep talk before he left. He had been observing the kids and he had known Tammy for years. He turned his chair around backwards and sat in front of the room.

"Kids—and, Tammy, I'll include you in this—we all have pivotal moments … times when a single decision can change the course of our lives and of others' lives. We often don't know the extent or the effect of these decisions. I have to make these types of judgments as an officer fairly often. Years ago, Preston sat me down at this very table and provided me the opportunity to turn my life around. He supported me and encouraged me. It made all the difference in the world."

He walked to the table leaned in and put both big hands flat on the table. "I want to compliment all of you for doing your best to make good decisions. Some decisions you have made lately are daring and dangerous. Risky things work for some people. What I see in this group sitting here is the potential for great things. Though some have been through tough times, you have chosen to grow from it and not be identified by the bad stuff. I expect you will make mistakes, but with wise counsel and good decisions, I expect great things from all of you. To the extent I can help within the parameters of my job and personally, don't hesitate to call me. To whom much is given, much is required."

As the sheriff stood to leave, Tammy noticed him wipe a tear from his eye. Between his heartfelt speech and Amber's intriguing comments about not writing everything, she was confused.

Amber asked, "Is there a place in town to get some photographs developed where the pictures will remain private?"

Tammy realized this might be a test. She said, "The drugstore sends film off for developing, but the busybody who works there looks through people's photos on a regular basis. I could develop the film myself, but I would feel compelled to use whatever photographs I saw to add to my story. The only other option is to send the photos off by mail and hope whoever develops them is not nosy."

Amber waited patiently.

Tammy said, "The drugstore is not a good option. I would be glad to develop them while I am developing our film. However, I will have to see all your pictures in order to develop them correctly. If there are things I should not see or you cannot trust me with, you should mail them off and take your chances there."

Ray and Don tried to remember what the pictures would show. They were not aware of the subtle interplay between Tammy and Amber.

Amber replied, "I would appreciate it if you would develop the pictures yourself and let no one else see them." She turned to the photographer and said, "No offense. If there are photos you need to use, we can discuss it with Ray and Don and see if we think it is a good idea. They were taken with my Instamatic, and I am sure they are not nearly as good as he takes. I wish I had thought of this before the sheriff left. Could you take a group picture of us? Tammy, would you come over and get in a picture?"

14

A day later, they finally got to do the real interview. Tammy had to change most of the questions she was planning to ask. She had planned some questions to put Amber on the spot and maybe trick her into saying things she did not mean. Now she approached the interview as if Amber were her sister.

The fire had to be a part of the discussion, but it did not have to be the focus.

Amber said, "I woke up coughing in the dark. Orange and yellow flames were all around the room, and my bed was on fire. The smells were awful. My eyes burned from the smoke and fumes. I dropped to the floor to escape the smoke and heat—as we had been taught in school—and the air was better. I made my way across the room and out into the hallway. I saw that my brother's room was completely in flames. I heard shouting from outside and hoped he had made it to safety with the others. The pain was so bad that I wanted to curl up and die. Somehow,

I slid down the stairs and crawled out the front door. A fireman grabbed me, and everything went black. Other than waking up a few times in terrible pain, I was kept sedated for a week."

Tammy stopped writing and said, "How bad were the burns?"

Amber rolled up her sleeve. "Please do not take a picture. Most of my torso is like this. A lot of my hair burned off, but it grew back okay. For some reason, it grew back a different shade of auburn in places. I was fortunate to have good doctors and nurses who took the time to help me heal. In the hospital, I decided to do all I could to get myself in shape. They had warned me about how much physical therapy was going to hurt. It was only through stretching the new tissue that I could regain full range of motion and flexibility. Whatever they told me to do, I did double. Some days, I cried for hours as I worked out. The heroes were the nurses and therapists who encouraged me and held me up. Because they pushed me, I came away with a determination to do whatever I set my mind to."

Tammy was writing furiously. "What about the actual escape from the cave?"

Amber emphasized the parts Don and Ray played in getting her water, batteries, and help. She detailed the journey through the small tunnel and how it felt to come face to face with a big skull with huge teeth. Realizing the bear had probably died from being trapped in the passage was enough to make her back out and get better prepared. She mentioned the note she had written on the cracked dirt floor.

Tammy said, "I can't believe your batteries kept failing."

Don said, "I removed them from old toys at my house because there were no new AA batteries to fit through the pipe."

Tammy said, "Continue with the story."

When Amber came to the part about getting tangled and trapped in the fence by her boot, both boys were on the edge of their seats. They had not heard that part.

Amber said, "There was some old fence wire I could not see. My boot went through the wire but would not come back out. Everything was black. I had to untie my boot—underwater, in the dark, and with wire wrapped around my ankle."

Ray and Don realized how close they had come to losing Amber. Neither could speak.

Tammy stopped her and asked, "What things went through your mind?"

Looking down, Amber replied quietly, "It was difficult to think clearly when I was running out of air. I thought of dying and losing my friends. Then I thought I had to take action with the little breath I had left. When the boot finally came off and my foot came free, the only place to go was back in the cave. I still had the rope in my hand so I pulled hard and followed the rope by feel only, deeper into the darkness. Going back into absolute darkness seemed to be my only hope."

Tammy said, "When you told the fire story earlier, you paused at your brother's door. You went back into the fire, didn't you? Going back is where you got most of the burns?"

Amber looked up with tears in her eyes. "No one knows I went in there. I couldn't find him. It was so hot and smoky. Whenever I stood up, I choked on the smoke. After searching and thinking he must have been rescued, I left the room. I was pretty much on fire when I came out the door. How did you know I left out that part?"

"You are not the kind of person to leave a friend behind if there are any other choices. Tell me more about the cave escape."

"I used the last bit of battery power in the flashlight to find the opening beside the wire and launched into daylight to fill my lungs with air."

Tammy said, "You mentioned another room with a cracked dirt floor. Tell me more."

"It was about fifty feet tall and shaped like a well. The passage I was in, made a four-foot round hole in the side. The dirt floor was about three feet down. The dirt was fine sediment. No rocks. I found a tiny bottle in the dirt."

Ray asked, "Did you see any passages in the top?"

"No, the flashlight was too dim. There might be another passage above where all the water came in at some point. Tammy, remember my earlier point? Some things don't need to be told just because you know them. This is a good example. You could print this, and there will be people swimming into the cave the next day. However, if we control the exploration, maybe no one will get hurt. I expect we will get some help soon with exploration. And, after all, it is private property."

Tammy agreed to hold off on the possibility that there were unexplored parts of the cave.

Ray said, "I've heard the cave called Preston's Cave, Dry Cave, and River Cave. Maybe it's time to give it a real name. Caves seem to be mostly named after the landowners or something found in the cave."

Tammy thought it was a great idea, and they started throwing out options. In the end, they decided the landowner should select a name. Don liked Preston Cave because it was what he had always heard it called. Tammy thought something catchier was needed. Amber agreed the name needed to be catchy but declined to call it "Amber Cave."

Ray said, "When Amber told about coming out of the river to get a breath of air, all I saw in my mind was King Triton. Gold trident spear raised high, coming out of the water. I think Trident Cave would be perfect.

Don said, "And the three of us are a trident too."

Amber said, "I like the name, but it would have more intrigue if no one knew why it was called Trident. Some might guess, but no one would know unless we told."

Tammy said, "You three are great. You are a writer's dream. You tell great stories and leave the reader in suspense. What's next?"

"Funny you should ask," said Amber. "We will have a few things for you to cover if you will be patient."

15

Amber met with Ray and Don to discuss how to recover the remainder of the gold and get it to the bank. The passage was still blocked, but it was only a matter of time before someone found the river access.

The sheriff was coming out later to meet her and give her some advice.

Ray wanted to show them something he had been working on. He produced three stout leather necklaces with strange somewhat crescent-shaped pendants. They looked like puzzle pieces. He arranged the necklaces in a circle and they snapped together perfectly.

Don and Amber looked at Ray like he was a magician.

He had hammered the solid brass coin into a smooth disk with few of the original stampings remaining. After drawing out the three identical interlocking designs, he sawed the coin into three equal parts and sanded and polished it for hours. They each had a memento of their adventure and their friendship. Their initials were engraved on the back of each pendant.

Amber said, "I love it."

Don said, "This is really cool. The pendant looks like the cave's main passage."

Amber examined the pendant, appreciating the talent of her friends even more. They put on the necklaces and tucked them into their shirts. There was no point in flaunting the treasures. The old brass coin did not have the value of the gold coins. It was not even a real coin. It was a proof sample off a new die for confederate twenty dollar gold pieces that never went into production.

*   *   *

They decided to go to the cave and bring out the gold and strongbox, which was hidden under the rocks. They brought the tractor with front-end loader to the front of the cave. When each load of gold was brought out, they hid it under the loader bucket under the weight of the tractor. Taking the tractor key to the house, they had lunch and waited for the lawyer to arrive.

16

That afternoon, an old pickup truck rolled up to the house. A well-dressed man stepped out and looked around.

Amber remained in the house until he stepped in her direction and said, "Miss Preston, I believe we have an appointment scheduled today. I am Frank, your attorney."

Amber stepped onto the porch and invited him to come up.

He continued to look around as he walked her way. On the porch, he held out his hand, formally introduced himself, and gave her his business card.

Amber asked to see his drivers' license.

He smiled. "Fair enough."

Amber said, "Can you only represent me—or can you represent more than one person at a time?"

"I can actually do both in most cases. Let's hear why you think you need a lawyer."

Amber explained how she wanted someone to advise her, Ray, and Don. She wanted each of them to share in whatever gold was recovered.

Frank said, "A few questions will need to be answered to determine the ownership of any recovered treasure. If you recover coins, they have a face value, a precious metal value, and a collectors' value. It will also have to be determined from whose property the valuables were recovered—and if they were stolen. Items could have been stolen and have an insurance claim paid on them. The same discovery must be done for gold and other valuables."

Amber read every word of the agreement Frank passed to her and signed it. "Can we start by getting this treasure, as you call it, into a bank? The sheriff suggested doing it publicly with an armored truck. What do you think?"

"I think you have an excellent idea. When can it be ready?"

Amber pulled a bar of gold from her hip pocket and slid it across the table. "We have a few boxes of these."

Frank's stern courtroom face broke into a wide grin.

Late in the afternoon, Amber had the gate closed when cars started lining the roadway by the gate. They moved aside as an armored truck crept to the front of the line.

Ray let Tammy in early to get some pictures for her exclusive story. They loaded the heavy wood box with gold bars, stacked more against the sides, and scattered glimmering gold coins on top.

Tammy helped with the staging. With the strongbox open, it made a great picture. After the pictures, the tractor's big bucket was lowered and pressed tightly to the ground, ready for the big reveal. Tammy could not stop smiling. She was mesmerized by the gold.

No mention was made about any other artifacts. The plan was to imply the gold had been found and would be safe in the bank.

Frank stood in front of the group and said, "Amber Preston and her friends, Ray and Don Spark, searched for and found a cache of gold that appears to be related to the Civil War. From the markings and dates, it appears to be authentic. We have not accurately calculated its value, but we have inventoried the coins and gold. As you will see, it is substantial. The exact numbers will be disclosed to the proper authorities. Questions of providence, ownership, taxes, and so forth will all be addressed soon. I am sure Uncle Sam will have an interest. The cave is on private property, and as we saw with the recent cave-in, which trapped Amber Preston, it is dangerous. Until the authorities have completed assessing the find, the cave is closed. No one is allowed inside without the expressed written permission of Amber Preston, the owner."

There was a lot of chatter in the crowd.

Frank said, "The entire farm was recently given to Amber Preston by her grandfather, and it is all legal and binding. I am sure many of you are thinking there could be more gold—and you would like to go find it yourself. More details will come out later, but I have been assured that all the gold was found. There were also manifests detailing the shipment. Here's a warning from the sheriff: 'Anyone trespassing in the cave will be arrested and prosecuted.'"

Frank deflected questions and called the armored truck guards forward.

Amber walked up to the tractor in front of the cave and started the engine. She raised the bucket in front, and the gold bars slid down into the dirt. Gold coins glistened on top of the piles of bars. Amber backed away and shut it down.

The guards approached the pile of gold with a two-wheeled cart and boxes. They loaded all the gold, and as the cameras flashed, they handed Amber papers to sign.

Frank smiled and shook his head. "The girl does know how to please a crowd."

The small group that was waiting at the bank was kept back by the sheriff's deputies.

17

"Lucky" Preston had been successful in business and land trading in Tennessee before the Gold Rush of 1859. He went west to the Colorado Territory to see if his luck would continue.

He bought and sold claims until he found a promising mine. Most miners didn't have the cash to keep a mine in operation. Lucky put his money into a mine and renamed it the Lucky Strike. He learned the mining trade quickly, and although he found a rich vein of gold, he only sold off and made public enough to keep the mine in operation. He had seen what happened when others thought you had hit the mother lode. They were soon digging next to you—or even on your claim. During three years of mining, he processed his excess gold and cast it into one-kilo bars.

Five strongboxes were full, and a bag of one hundred, twenty-dollar gold pieces topped the fifth box. Lucky put a certificate of origin in each box and consigned the entire lot to his nephew: Nathaniel Preston.

Tennessee was a long way from Colorado. He labeled the boxes as machine parts and put the boxes in small mining equipment crates. Labeled as such, he hoped to get it successfully by rail to Memphis to his nephew, who was in the Confederate Army. He told Nathaniel by letter where in Memphis the mining equipment would be located and about the coins if he needed to pay for storage.

18

Tennessee, 1865

Sergeant Nathaniel Preston and his four men were running for their lives. They had received an important shipment in Memphis, Tennessee, from Nathaniel's uncle in the Colorado Territory. Though machine parts were listed on the manifest, they suspected—by the weight—it might be gold. For security, they had not been told the true nature of the mission.

The following week, they fought their way through bandits and deserters. Mid-way across Tennessee, they received word from a scout about a small group of Union cavalrymen who were a two days' ride behind them. The air was cold, and it looked like snow. They hurried to beat the snow and avoid leaving tracks. The cavalry traveled light and rode hard. Nathaniel's men had two additional packhorses and six hundred pounds of cargo. They were going to a cave with a secret room that was known only to him and his brother.

All his men were tired and injured from run-ins with highwaymen. That late in the war, there were deserters everywhere. People were desperate and would do most anything to survive. The war had taken a toll on both sides. Nathaniel knew getting the shipment delivered was critical to the outcome of the war. The shipment was not going to fall into the hands of the Union soldiers.

After meeting briefly with Nathaniel's brother, they hobbled and limped into the cave. With ropes, they dragged the heavy strongboxes back to the first room. It was round and had one way in—and no way out. Nathaniel directed them to go beyond that room to a place where a ladder was propped against the wall. They hauled the strongboxes up the ladder and into a shallow passage against the roof. In another room, they stacked the boxes on one side and made camp to wait out their pursuers. Even if it took a few days, they needed time to rest and recover. They were wounded and were barely able to climb the ladders.

Nathaniel's brother hid the horses far from the entrance and moved the ladder to another passage in the cave. Nathaniel used rocks from the inside of the small passage to make a thin temporary wall over the tunnel entrance to the main passage. They were hidden, but they only had food and water for about a week.

Nathaniel's brother was not surprised when the Union cavalry arrived a few days later. He was glad he had written about Nathaniel and sent a letter to a friend before the cavalry arrived. After the soldiers found the extra horses, they interrogated him. He finally told them they had put the boxes in two boats and floated down the river where they were to meet with troops in a few days. He said Nathaniel had traded the horses for two small flat-bottomed boats. The interrogation did not end well for Nathaniel's brother.

After five days in the cave, the men were feverish and running out of food. Nathaniel was in command and had insisted on staying one more day. Private Deal was a thin man and had not been injured badly. He explored a passage that ended in water. He could not swim, and it was the middle of winter. He refilled his canteen and struggled back to the room.

Two of the soldiers were nearly dead, and another was unable to walk.

Private Deal started climbing the ladder to break through the rocks to leave. Nathaniel ordered him to stop, but Deal—half crazed with hunger and fear—fired his pistol.

Nathaniel fell to the floor.

Deal went over to the strongbox and took out a few gold bars and filled his pockets with gold coins. He left the full canteen for the injured man, took a rifle, and climbed the ladder. Seconds later, he hauled the ladder into the passage. After replacing the rocks over the opening to the passage, he climbed down the ladder and took it out of the cave. The room in the cave became a death chamber that would not be seen again for seven decades.

19

Tennessee, 1934

Nat Preston's wife, Nellie, was obsessed with finding the lost treasure in the cave. She got ideas about where the gold might be and dug for days. For the six years, they had been married, Nat worked hard on the farm. They had survived, but he wanted children. He longed to have kids running around on the farm. As far as Nat was concerned, if they did not want to farm, they could work in the nearby factories. He wanted to teach his kids how to hunt and fish. He even dreamed of having grandkids.

Nellie had other ideas. She cooked and cleaned occasionally—and she searched for gold. Every rumor or old story got her excited again—and she went back in the cave. She had a carbide light, a pick, and a shovel. She reasoned the soldiers did not have time to do more than dig a hole and bury the gold. Though it had been seven decades since the soldiers buried the treasure, she dug at every mound or sunken place in the cave. She found buttons or scraps of steel and concluded they were from the Civil War troops.

Nat tried to get her to start a family.

She said, "Once we find the gold, we will go to the city, buy a big house, and start a family."

When Nat came in from the fields one evening, he could not find Nellie. He went to the cave to find her. Donning a carbide headlamp and carrying some equipment, he ventured into the cave. He periodically shouted to see if she would answer. Years earlier, she always told him which direction she was going. After a while, she left without even leaving a note. Nat followed the main passage past the round room and found a ladder. Rocks were scattered along the main passageway, blocking the normally clear walkway.

He climbed the ladder and found a small passageway near the ceiling. Most of the debris was cleared out, and he could see into a room about eight feet away. There was light dancing around in the room. Nat called out to Nellie, but she did not answer. He crawled into the small passage and found her walking around the room, looking at Confederate uniforms. She had gold bars in each hand and was chanting. The floor was about ten feet below, and there was no ladder. He called out again—more gently. She stopped. In a daze, she stared blankly at him through tears. Sensing something was wrong, he asked her to come out to see him. She said something about her grandfather and pointed to the remains of a Confederate soldier. Nat asked her if she had food and water. She shook her head. He had a canteen and pitched it down near her feet. She stared at it. Knowing he had to rescue her, he told her he was going to get food, rope, and another ladder.

Much earlier in the day, when Nellie discovered the room, a large pit had been dug in the soft dirt near a wall. While Nat was gone, Nellie finished what she started. Reverently she removed the remnants of the clothing from each skeleton and put the bones in the grave. She figured the soldiers had dug it either to bury the gold or to bury those who did not survive. She piled all the bones carefully in the pit and said a prayer. She went back to each uniform and straightened the tattered cloth as best she could. In her mind, they had protected the gold for her for seven decades and deserved a fitting burial. As she made her last trip into the pit, she put a gold bar on the pile of bones. She felt a sharp pain in her arm. Her chest hurt, and she had to sit down.

When Nat returned, she was collapsed in the grave. He tried to revive her, but it was too late. She had passed after finding the gold she had obsessed over for six years. He said a prayer and lamented losing his wife and the family he would never have. After a time of grieving, he buried her near the treasure she had died for, filled in the grave, and smoothed out the floor. She had really been gone for years. The fever took her from him long ago. He pocketed a handful of gold bars, climbed out, and dragged the ladder behind him.

The next day, he returned and built the wall in the passage. He also buried a warning in a bottle.

20

Preston's Farm, 1973

When Amber was twelve, she visited Preston during the summer. Amber, Ray, and Don were exploring the woods near the house while Preston was gone. A fancy car drove to the house, and a man with slicked-back hair got out. He looked around and called in the direction of the house.

The kids quietly watched from the cover of the woods, knowing Preston was not home.

The man craned his neck to see if anyone was around, and then he walked toward the fence where the cattle were grazing and stopped at the water trough. After he looked furtively around, he pulled out a small bottle and unscrewed the top.

Amber was accustomed to being around someone who drank a lot and thought the man had stopped there to sneak a drink. To her surprise, he dumped the entire bottle into the water trough. Replacing the lid, he jogged back to his car and sped away.

As the car neared the end of the driveway, he threw something into the ditch. The car gained speed and was soon out of sight.

"Who was that?" asked Amber.

"No idea," Ray replied. "What did he pour in the water trough? He was sneaking around like he was doing something wrong.'"

Don said, "He did look suspicious. Let's go have a look."

They went to the water trough, and the water looked the same.

"Could have been whiskey," said Ray.

Don said, "What if it was poison?"

Amber said, "Why would he poison the cows?"

The curious cows were approaching, probably thinking they were about to be fed.

Don said, "We can't let them drink—in case it's poison. Keep them away, Ray."

Amber said, "While you keep watch over the water trough, I'll run to the road and see if he threw out the bottle." She searched the ditch, but all she found were some cola bottles. When she looked outside the ditch, she found a small capped bottle with a tiny amount of liquid in the bottom. Thinking there might be fingerprints, she used a piece of paper from the roadside to grab the bottle. She ran back to the boys to show them the evidence. *This is beginning to feel like a Nancy Drew adventure. Preston needs to know about this.*

Ray and Don drove the cattle out of the field and locked the gate. While they waited on Preston, they tried to remember the type of car the man had been driving. They only remembered it was big and shiny, had two doors, and was green.

When Preston arrived an hour later, all three kids were on his porch.

They were excited and talking all at once, but Preston got them to tell the story from the beginning.

Preston examined the bottle without touching it and thanked them for watching out for his cattle. Then he called the sheriff to see if he wanted to take the bottle and have it checked out.

As he walked the boys toward home, they stopped, drained, and rinsed the tank again. He told the boys to go home and promised to let them know what he found out.

The sheriff came by and put the bottle in a plastic bag.

Amber was pleased. *This is like a TV show.*

A week later, the sheriff came back. The bottle had no fingerprints. It had been wiped clean, which was very suspicious. Inside the bottle, there were a few drops of strychnine, a very strong poison.

The sheriff said, "Preston, can you think of any reason someone would want to poison your cattle?"

They talked for a while, but neither man could think of a reason. Everyone in the community liked Preston, and he had no enemies he knew about. The man with slicked-back hair and a light green two-door shiny car was their only clue.

21

Preston's Farm, 1975

There was another old house on the Preston farm. The small house had a ladder to a tiny upstairs area. The wood house with a tin roof was usually referred to as the sharecropper house. It stood on stacks of rocks and had small front and back porches. No one had lived there for twenty years and it was nearly overgrown with bushes and trees. The old fireplace and chimney had been built from rocks in the fields.

There was a legend about the old house. A wild lady who was living there went berserk. When her husband came home one night and climbed the ladder through the little square hole in the floor, she split his head with an axe.

Ray and Don had told Amber the legend of the old house when she was twelve to scare her. Now they retold the story with lots of exaggerated details as the three sat around the campfire by the river in front of the cave. The fog rolled slowly down the river on that cool summer evening. It carried the scent of the surrounding farmlands. The campfire was great for the boys. For Amber, the smell of a burning wood still brought back memories of the fire. Each time was less vivid. She healed more each day, but still hated fire.

They roasted marshmallows on long sticks and occasionally sacrificed one to the fire. Don called them burnt offerings. Ray told story after story, and Amber asked if the one about the old sharecropper house was true.

Ray put the flashlight under his chin, illuminating his face from below, and said in a scary voice, "Let's go find out."

They grabbed flashlights and walked into the woods making their way through the low brush and onto the front porch. Ray used a walking stick to push away limbs and clear out spider webs.

The house smelled musty and old. The front door was open, and the floor was littered with bottles, paper, and old cooking pans. As they shined their lights around the room, they saw broken windows and a small back door. Something smelled dead. They could not tell where the smell came from, but it was bad.

Ray said, "It might be the body of the dead husband!"

Don said, "It has been forty years. That's a long time to be stinking."

Amber said, "Where is the stairway?"

Don said, "There are no stairs. See the ladder near the wall? A tight squeeze through the floor is the only way up or down."

"Who is going first?" asked Amber.

Don and Ray said they had already been there—so maybe Amber should go first.

Not wanting to appear afraid, Amber said, "I'm not scared." She headed for the ladder.

Don grabbed the handle of a nearby pan, and Ray tightened his grip on the walking stick.

The ladder was very narrow, and it angled out slightly toward the middle of the room.

As Amber's arm with the flashlight came through the floor, her hand pushed into something soft. She climbed higher, and as her head came through the floor, she heard a loud crack. The house and ladder shook. She dropped like a rock and landed between the ladder and the wall. Her legs were on either side, and a terrified look was on her face.

Ray and Don had timed it perfectly. The old curtain hanging near the hole in the floor was a great touch. Hitting the wall and ladder with the pan and walking stick made her think the axe was coming down! They had been planning it for a week.

They would have rolled on the floor and laughed, but the floor was far too filthy. Still struggling to get their composure, they helped Amber stand up.

She started laughing and agreed they had pulled a good one on her. She picked up the flashlight and went back up the ladder. The black stains near the top of the ladder cascaded down each rung. She bent over as she made it to the upstairs room. It had an angled roof and bare rafters on both sides. She could only stand straight in the middle. The floor felt very weak and sagged deeply when she walked. Something in the corner caught her eye. Pushing an old bottle aside with her flashlight, she picked up a small marble. It was not perfectly round, and it was opaque. It felt like it was made of stone. She put it in her pocket as a souvenir for the memory shelf.

22

Preston and Sheila came back from the Smoky Mountains when they heard Amber had been trapped in the cave. By the time they got back to the farm, the gold was in the bank and the kids were safe at home. They wanted to hear the entire story, and they invited everyone over for dinner.

As Amber and Sheila cooked, Sheila pretended to be distressed that Amber did not have any fresh kangaroo to cook! They laughed and had a great time.

During the meal, they talked about the trip to the Smoky Mountains and how Amber would start school in the fall.

Preston said, "Let's get to the big story. Who wants to start off the story of grand adventures?"

Amber said, "Since I talked to my lawyer today, I probably have more current information than anyone else. Frank took the manifest from the strongbox. He did some research and found out the gold originated in the Colorado Territory. The gold was shipped east and signed over to Nathaniel Preston. The gold was actually passed into his name specifically. It technically became his gold.

"He and his men transported it from Memphis to the cave. According to Frank, this cave was on the property owned by Nathaniel and his brother. The gold came from his uncle. For years, the farm and cave belonged to Preston, and now to me."

Preston said, "It seems I have given away the farm to my granddaughter—and she has a substantial windfall to boot. I could not be more proud. Almost everyone in this county, including me, searched for gold, and it took you three kids to find it. How did you do it?"

Amber said, "Before we get into our adventures, you need to know a little more about what we found. I talked to Frank about this today, and he is helping us find the best way to proceed. Who knew a fourteen-year-old would need a high-priced lawyer to stay out of trouble? In the rubble of the passage we dug out, there was a bottle with a note. The writer said we should fill it back in, and forget we got that far. It said he had lost his wife and hope of a family. We kept digging. When Don broke through, there was a room. Inside were four Civil War uniforms, five strongboxes of gold, a Bible, a notebook, some coins, a sword, and four rifles."

The adults were speechless. They had only heard about the gold.

Amber said, "I also found the skeleton of a bear in the passage I escaped through. To escape the cave, I had to dive underwater and swim through a passage to the river."

Sheila walked over to Amber and pulled her into a tight embrace. Britney and Ben did the same for Ray and Don.

Britney said, "We knew it was probably traumatic being stuck in the cave for those hours. We had no idea about the soldiers. I am so sorry you all had to experience the whole scene."

Don said, "It was a little spooky at first, but we all worked together to make the best of it. At least they didn't stink! There was not much there besides the uniforms."

Preston said, "Now I can see why Frank is still involved. The authorities will want to investigate this and make sure it is not a crime scene. I believe you mentioned five strongboxes of gold! I heard on the news that all the gold was found."

Ray said, "It is true. All the gold was found, but we don't have it all out yet. Frank worded it carefully to help discourage people from going into the cave and looking for more."

As Amber shared the details about the discovery, they began to eat again. The questions went back and forth until everyone had a good understanding of where they were.

Everyone was wondering how to get the remainder of the gold out if the hidden passage was blocked by a big rock. The next concern was timing. When should they tell the sheriff about the Civil War uniforms and the bullet holes?

23

Preston and Amber met with Frank and the sheriff the next day. The sheriff was a little upset that he was not told about the Civil War soldiers sooner. He understood why Amber had waited and was glad Frank had advised her to share the information.

Trying to figure the best way into the room to recover the artifacts was tough. Amber said going through the river and the narrow passage would work, but getting the corpses out—if they found any—would be nearly impossible. Though it would be expensive, it might be better to drill a small passage near floor level and bring everything into the main passage.

Amber told the sheriff about the other boxes of gold—and she wanted to know how to keep someone from going in through the river and stealing it.

24

The river was low, and the spring rains were mostly over. Two scruffy men and a big fellow with slicked-back hair floated down the river in a flat-bottomed boat. They had fishing poles, but they did not seem interested in fishing. Victor Deal was wearing a leisure suit because he was the brains of the group and did not plan on getting dirty. The other men were the Crum brothers.

If Victor needed something illegal done, he called the Crums. Always needing extra money, Victor could depend on them to do most anything.

The men stayed close to the river bank as they floated down near the clearing. In the distance the bluff loomed over the river and the dark shadow of the cave opening was prominent by the clearing.

Victor said, "They think putting up a few No Trespassing signs can keep me from getting what is mine."

The boat scraped against the rocks as they reached the bluff and grabbed a bush to stop. Trying to look casual, they scanned the river for any passing boats or fishermen. An occasional canoe or kayak would come into view far around a bend.

All three men focused on the water between the boat and the rocks of the bluff. As they all looked over the boat dipped and almost capsized. Gallons of water flooded into the boat. Overreacting, they shifted to the other side of the boat, but even more water cascaded in. They frantically scooped out water to avoid sinking. Hissing in stage whispers, they accused each other of nearly tipping the boat. Once they were out of danger of sinking, they let the boat inch down the river.

"What are we looking for?" one of the bearded men asked as he kept scooping out water with a can. "They already found all the gold and took it away in an armored truck."

Deal said, "I think they got part of the gold. It would be too much of a coincidence for all the gold to be removed—and then the girl gets stuck. Also they only brought out one strongbox to go in the armored truck. Some of the gold was not in a strongbox. I know there is more gold! And it is mine. There must be a cave opening into the river below the water level. When the girl appeared at the mouth of the cave, she was soaking wet. Look for an opening back under the rocks. How deep is it here?"

The bearded man with the limp reached his paddle down toward the bottom until his arm was under water. He said, "It must be more than eight feet. I can't touch the bottom."

They kept checking the rocks as they went down the river until they had gone past the bluff where the riverbank was lower.

Victor said, "Let's go back and look again. It's got to be there."

They worked their way back upriver, pulling on branches and pushing their paddle under the bank, feeling for an opening.

Halfway along the bluff, the paddle pushed into an opening about five feet underwater. They tried again and found an opening a few feet upriver. The murky water made it nearly invisible from the boat. Holding a nearby branch, Victor pulled the boat over to the bluff and made a small stack of rocks to mark the spot. He hoped no one would notice the tiny marker before they came back for the gold.

They pushed the boat a few feet away from the bank, and stared at the river bottom. Something looked like the end of a rope coiled just inside the cave opening. As it began to get dark, the Crum brothers paddled back upriver. Victor sat in the middle seat and cursed them for getting him wet. It was a long way back to the bridge where they had parked their truck with the camper top and the realtor's shiny rental car.

25

The sheriff talked with some state officials to get some guidance in case they found bodies or the skeletons of the soldiers believed to have died in the cave. They discussed burial costs and recovery costs for artifacts or remains. The sheriff had already determined Nellie was likely the name of the lady who was lost in the cave in the 1930s. He suspected she was somehow involved after reading the note in the bottle.

To recover the soldier's remains, the plan was to bore a tunnel in from the main passage. The owner of a concrete core drilling company said he could drill through ten feet of limestone in a day. He argued the bodies had been in there for at least a hundred years—another day or so would not matter. Because this was a high profile job and he would get publicity, he agreed to do it for the thousand dollars Amber offered.

26

After all the excitement about gold in the cave, more and more people were on the river and sneaking onto the property. The sheriff posted a deputy at the mouth of the cave day and night until they could recover the remains.

After a greeting to the deputy stationed by the cave, Amber walked down to the edge of the bluff to see if her marker was still there. It was a rough climb to stay on the edge of the bluff without sliding into the river. The weeds were higher, and it was a little more difficult to see the marker she had made. As she looked around, she spotted a tiny stack of rocks. It was recent because it was sitting on top of green leaves. Someone had found the cave passage. She felt sick when she realized someone could be in the cave now and no one would know.

Amber hurried back up the path, slipping once and nearly falling into the river. She cautioned the deputy to keep an eye out for boats. At the house, she called her lawyer for advice.

Frank said they could not restrict passage because the river was public. "It is also illegal to make any kind of trap to harm someone trying to get access."

The thought had crossed her mind. The memory of tangling in the old fence wire was scary enough to know she did not want to put anyone else in danger.

Once word got out about the gold and the latest revelation about Civil War soldiers, a lady from *National Geographic* wanted to write a story about the discovery and the history of the soldiers. She said it was important to document everything as early as possible.

Frank actually thought it was a good idea. He had verified her identity and was familiar with her work. Frank suggested putting together a team to document everything. He suggested Tammy, Scarlet from *National Geographic*, the sheriff, Ray, Don, Amber, and Preston.

Amber wasted no time asking Scarlet if *National Geographic* could send in divers with cameras. Scarlet, sensing a big story, was on the phone within minutes. In an hour, she had three divers pulled off an exploratory project near Oak Ridge, Tennessee, and headed to the Preston farm.

Even as Amber was making plans for the dive team, the Crum brothers tired of dealing with "Double-Dealing Victor Deal." He offered to give them each a gold bar to go in and get the gold.

Gerald Crum said, "He acted like the gold was already his, and he was just paying us to go fetch it for him. Now that we found the entrance, we can get the gold for ourselves. We can take the gold, get in the truck, and never see Tennessee again."

As night fell, the Crum brothers prepared to dive into the cave. This time, they had a trolling motor, and paddles. Tonight they would double-cross Victor and give him a dose of his own medicine.

Harold Crum brought a mask and snorkel. He had no idea how long he would have to swim under the rock, but the girl made it without a mask. They searched for the stack of rocks, but they were gone. They shoved the paddle under the bank until they found the cave. It concerned them that someone had found their marker—maybe they were too late.

They tied the boat to a small tree on the river's edge. From the side of the boat, on another rope, they lowered a battery-powered light to the bottom. It lit the river bottom at the mouth of the cave, which made it easy to find the way out.

Harold Crum tied the end of a rope he was taking to the boat, and told his brother he would be back in thirty minutes. "If I am not back, come looking for me."

27

The core driller was anxious as he got started. It was the highest-profile job he had ever done. Photographers were taking pictures and filming with big spotlights. When he warned them that the process could take a long time, they stopped filming and waited.

For the job, he used a twenty-four-inch coring tool. After every few inches, the saw was pulled out—and the core was broken out with a jack hammer. Then he drilled deeper and repeated the slow process. He promised a smooth bore right into the room if the kid's estimates on the room's location were accurate.

The noise was deafening and constant. Water was circulated onto the cutting surfaces to keep the bits cool as they chewed through the limestone.

* * *

Harold Crum cleared his mask and dropped down below the boat. With his light, he could see into the cave. He went back to the surface and took a few breaths. After confirming with Gerald, he dropped down to the bottom and pushed off toward the cave opening.

He immediately snagged in the fence wire. When he hit the wire, it was such a surprise that he lost some breath. Once he got free of the rusty tangle, he was out of breath. He pushed up fast and was still under the edge of the cave opening. He banged his head on the rock as he surfaced. Blood ran down his head and into his beard. He was barely able to stay conscious after the impact.

Gerald easily dragged his brother into the boat. He listened to what Harold described about the fence inside the cave and decided to dive in Harold's place for the gold. He put on the mask and snorkel, tied a rope around his waist, and went over the signals with his brother. Struggling to slide over the side of the boat without bringing in even more water, he accidentally dropped his light. He swam down and looked around for the light. He saw the wire and a shoe hanging from the fencing. A rope was on the bottom. To his left, he saw a triangular opening he could easily swim through. He surfaced to confirm that he had all his gear, and that his brother was okay. He dropped down, kicked, and swam through the opening into the cave. Feeling overhead, he swam until he saw the silver reflection of the water in the pool. Taking a grateful breath, he gazed back toward the boat. He saw the light on the bottom clearly.

Gerald detached the rope from his waist and pulled on it twice as a signal to his brother that he was in the cave and okay. He shouldered his gear and walked in search of the gold. The headlamp on his helmet left his hands free to carry equipment and gold. When he came to a fork, he chose left. After a few moments, he came to a circular room with cracks in the dirt floor. The room was about fifty feet tall. Something was written in the dirt: "Amber Preston, 1975: Posted No Trespassing! You have been warned!"

After checking the room thoroughly, he decided it was a dead end. He backtracked to the fork in the path and heard a rumbling sound. Amber's words on the dirt floor bothered him.

Gerald decided it must be the right tunnel. The passage was only knee-high. He took off his pack, hooked it to his belt, and dragged it along. As the angle got steeper, crawling became more difficult. The sound got louder, and the passage got smaller and tighter. His pack started snagging on things. He had to go backward several times to unhook it.

The passage was so small and steep that he could barely move forward. Once the passage finally leveled out, he could only crawl with his arms forward and pushing with his toes. His light dragged off his head from contact with the ceiling. Because his arms were stretched out in front, he could not retrieve his light.

Pushing backwards, he wedged tighter in the passage. His fingers finally hooked the dropped head lamp. Shining the light, he saw bones ahead and all around him. Vertebrae, large rib bones, and bones of all sizes littered the passage. He thought about being trapped. His breath came faster, and fear crept in like the cold he felt all around. He tried to move forward, but his pack was wedged under him. Moving backward wedged him even tighter. Realizing why the skeleton was in the passage, the cave seemed to tighten around him. The vibration continued. As his fear mounted, he wondered if the drilling he heard was for blasting. It did not sound far away. It sounded and felt like it was getting closer.

*   *   *

Gerald was right, not sixty feet away, the drilling continued. The driller brought in another crew to keep the machine running. The saw was carbide, and as long as it was kept cool, it did not have to be changed or sharpened. They drilled, pulled out core samples, and drilled again. The cores of rock were moved down the passageway to make room for more. Some of the round sections were stacked in the main passage like stools or benches to sit on. The operator announced, "Maybe just a few hours to go!"

28

The *National Geographic* divers arrived and were brought up to speed on the river access. They stopped in town and enjoyed some locally famous cheeseburgers and talked with Frank and Scarlet about the plan.

The restaurant owner said, "Phone call, Frank! It's the sheriff!"

Frank went to the office to get the phone.

The sheriff said, "I got a radio call from the deputy. A man in a boat came to the riverbank and was bleeding. He said his partner had gone into the water entrance and had not come out for three hours. Do you have the divers with you?"

*　*　*

Frank, Scarlet, and the three divers sped to the farm, and Amber met them at the cave. While they got into their gear, Amber filled them in on every detail she remembered.

"Anyone much bigger than me won't make it through the skeleton passage. There still a lot of bones to crawl through. The tight spot where the bear died is likely where the man was stuck." Looking at the smallest diver, Amber said, "That makes it easy to decide who tries to make the rescue."

The small diver said, "I don't know if you are trying to scare us or just make us wonder what the heck we are getting ourselves into."

She told them about the wire and the correct passage to take. Since they might have to pull the intruder out by his feet, Amber recommended a 150-foot rope.

This went beyond the normal scope of diving and taking pictures. The least experienced diver manned the boat, and the bigger man photographed and assisted. The thin diver attempted the rescue.

Tammy negotiated some free pictures and videos for her local story.

Scarlet wrote background for the magazine article.

29

The boring continued with hopes of breaking through soon. Since there was no actual measurement of the wall thickness, they were only guessing. The estimate of ten feet came and went, and the drilling continued.

The drill started jerking and then settled back to its normal grind. The operator pulled back the bit to examine the teeth. A few looked like they had hit something very hard. Removing the core section, they found black glasslike rock, in the limestone. The driller pointed to the black area and told the cameramen it was obsidian. They rolled the core section to the side and kept drilling. The damaged teeth slowed the process slightly, but they drilled on.

* * *

A hundred feet away, the divers prepared to attempt a rescue. The two divers wore wetsuits more for padding than water exposure. They carried lights, ropes, a first aid kit, cameras, rations, and water. In the position where Amber directed them, they tied off the boat and dropped a light to the bottom. Knowing the risk of hypothermia to the trapped thief, they hurried to get inside.

The divers made their way through the opening beside the submerged fence. They emerged in the pool of water and shined their lights around the cave. They removed the scuba gear and piled it on the sloping dirt beside the water. Dressed in boots and helmets from a dry bag they switched on another camera. Tying off the rope, they moved quickly to the fork in the passage Amber had described. The first thing they noticed was the grinding machine sound coming from the small passage.

Pulling the rope behind, the smaller diver crawled along the passage. The diver could see something blocking the passage. He called out to what looked like boots ahead but got no response. Snaking closer, he grabbed one of the boots, shook it and called out. An animal like moan filled the passage.

The diver tied the rope securely around the man's boots. The pack was wedged under the man's knees and the strap was snagged on a rock. Pulling the strap eventually, freed the pack. Although this seemed to loosen the man from the rock wall, he made no effort to move.

The diver backed away and shouted the situation to his companion. He dreaded dragging the man a hundred feet back to the fork. With both divers pulling on the rope, the man's feet began to move. They pulled in tandem, and the body moved more freely. Groans came from the trapped man as he was dragged face-down through the passage.

When they reached the fork, the man was beginning to come around. They untied his feet and got blankets and heating pads out of the dry bag. They treated his scratches and cuts with antibiotic cream. As he warmed, they gave him water and hot coffee from a thermos. The divers knew enough about hypothermia to know this fellow was lucky to be alive.

Gerald Crum neither told his name nor admitted his intentions. He only said he was curious about the reports of gold.

The divers documented everything on film and still pulled off the rescue. One diver proposed a toast with a thermos of hot coffee. "Here's to a successful rescue and the beginning of an interesting documentary." The divers clinked cups but Gerald stared blankly into his own.

The large diver decided to send a report to the diver on the boat. He wrote an update and said they would bring the victim out when he was warmer. He tied it to the middle of the rope to the boat in a watertight envelope. Two pulls on the rope signaled the man on the boat to haul in the line.

When he returned to the fork in the passage, the small diver was preparing to go back in the Skeleton Passage to take a picture of the room, if he could get through. As a precaution, he tied a rope to his foot and started into the passage. As he neared the bones, the passage got tight. He kept the camera extended in front and his arms stretched out, and he squeezed through. The grinding sound was much louder.

From his high vantage point, he filmed the room. Panning the camera all around, he captured images of unusual soldier uniforms, boxes that looked very old, and guns against the wall. The noise of the drilling crew was deafening and made it hard to concentrate on the images. He shifted the light and camera toward some motion across the room. About three feet above the floor, water was spraying through an opening in the rock!

When the drill broke through, light flooded in. The tool was backed out, and the debris was cleared. The photographer's timing was perfect. He kept the camera rolling. With his free hand he fumbled with a still camera to capture some photographs. He whispered, "If these pictures come out, I will be famous."

Amber crawled through the core hole and shined a light around.

He took another great picture. She scanned the room and did not even acknowledge his glaring lights from his perch above the room.

The sheriff came after Amber but barely fit through. Then the local reporter, Tammy, came in and set up a tripod. She seemed confused at the sight of the lights and the young diver perched at the top of the room. The diver filmed it all. Because she was cute, he took a close up of Tammy.

The noise subsided, and the quiet in the crypt seemed eerie. The sheriff looked over the scene. One soldier's uniform had a paper sticking partially out of the pocket. There were no skulls, and the uniforms seemed to be mostly empty.

Tammy took a picture as the sheriff removed the paper. In very poor penmanship, someone had scribbled:

All are dead now but me. Private Deal disobeyed orders to stay put. He shot Sergeant Nathaniel Preston, took some of the gold, and left. He walled up the opening and left me to die here. I am not able to walk or climb out. If you find this someday, know Private Deal is a murderer and a thief.
Private

The name was faded and unreadable.

30

Gerald Crum recovered quickly with warm blankets, water, and food. While the thin diver was gone, Gerald decided it was time to act. With the diver not looking, he hit him over the head with a flashlight and knocked him out cold. He went to the water's edge and put on a set of diving equipment. He had been in the military a few years before and knew how to use scuba gear.

He gathered everything he needed and slipped into the water. To help avoid detection, he did not exhale bubbles as he swam out of the cave and beneath the boat. He swam across the river unseen and stopped at a vantage point where he could see across to the cave main entrance. He saw his boat tied beneath a tree across the river. He swam over to the boat. There was a crowd at the cave and lots of noise. He slipped into the boat unseen, untied the line, and started the little electric trolling motor.

He moved quickly upriver to the bridge, dragged his boat into the back of his camper, and left.

*   *   *

The sheriff declared the cave a crime scene and had everyone move out of the room. He examined the uniforms of the soldiers. Unsure if there were any remains in the uniforms, he proceeded as if they were bodies. The sergeant uniform had a bullet hole through his breast pocket and out the back. The sheriff did not share the contents of the note or the name of the assailant.

Tammy was elated. Not realizing she was saying it out loud, Amber heard her say, "Not only is there gold—this is a murder scene. Could this get any better?"

Amber eased close to her, "Remember what we talked about. I believe there is a big story here. We need to talk before reporting too much. I am sure the sheriff will want you to be considerate of his investigation. Also, if you play your cards right, you and Scarlet can work together on this."

*   *   *

A tug came on the small diver's rope. He shouted back that he was on his way. Turning around at the entrance to the room, he shouted to the sheriff, "I am headed back to help take the victim to the boat. Can you have a deputy meet us at the river's edge near the mouth of the cave?"

When he arrived at the fork in the tunnels, he found his fellow diver recovering from a knock on the head. Moving to the water's edge, they quickly figured out what had happened. They hoped their diving buddy on the boat was okay.

They gathered their gear, but they only had one tank and mask. The small diver went first, taking a light load of gear. He was surprised to find the third diver waiting patiently in the boat, unaware the would-be thief had escaped beneath him.

The diver quickly filled him in and got the extra diving gear to take back to the cave. Once inside, the big diver eased the strap over his bruised head. Though it was painful, he headed for the boat with a load. The small diver made one last check of the area and gathered all the remaining gear, including the rope Amber had left tied to a rock. After depositing the equipment in the boat, he went down one last time to retrieve Amber's shoe from the wire. They took a final picture and moved to the clearing near the mouth of the cave.

The deputy who met them there was surprised to have no one to arrest. The man who had come to camp bleeding and asking for help for his friend had disappeared too. Since he had not been caught trespassing in the cave, they did not have any reason to hold him. In fact, no one had even asked Harold Crum's name.

31

State officials told the sheriff, "Since no bodies were found and no one could possibly be living who could have committed the murder mentioned in the note, there is no crime to investigate." The documentation Frank researched about providence of the gold was enough for the sheriff to release the cave back to the owner. Amber was free to recover the gold and artifacts.

At Frank's suggestion, they returned to the cave. As the *National Geographic* team documented the room with pictures and video, they recovered the gold, guns, and everything except the uniforms. The armored truck was called in again, and with pictures and much fanfare, they hauled the strongboxes of gold, to the bank. Other artifacts were for a museum. Uniforms were left in place for further research. The story was sensational, and people began to speculate about the value of the gold in the truck.

32

After things were settled about the gold discovery, *National Geographic* agreed to fund an exploration project to see if there were more passages that held more clues about the remains of the soldiers. They brought in loaders and hauled out the breakdown in the main passage so there was no longer a need to crawl. Amber talked them into excavating a path along the river bluff and back to the water access. From there, they cut away the stone, accessed the cavern above the waterline, and installed a steel gate. Even with the water entrance blocked, there was now easy access through the newly bored passage. Ben commissioned a local welder to make and install a gate blocking the crypt access.

Some explorers were intrigued by the cracked floor of the pit and dug down into the soft dirt. Using screens for sifting archeological relics, they began to find artifacts. There were beads, clay pot shards, and tiny ceramic figurines.

After discovering these relics, the kids began to call this the Sacrificial Pit. Ray suspected there was another large passage above where American Indians or cavemen dropped things as sacrifices. They decided to have experienced climbers scale the wall with ropes and pitons. If there was a passage, they would fix a permanent cable ladder to the top and along the side so explorers could ascend easily. Amber arranged for three climbers to bring equipment and meet them at the cave the next day.

They scaled the vertical wall in about an hour. At the top, a curved side passage was large enough to stand comfortably. As tempting as it was to explore, the climbers were instructed to only take pictures, mount the ladder, and climb back down. What they saw was much more than a passage. They took several excellent pictures before they reluctantly climbed back down. The climbers were excited when they returned and asked if they could explore. When the request was denied, they gave the camera back to the *National Geographic* explorers, packed their gear, and made their way out of the cave.

* * *

Tammy was working with Scarlet, and she allowed the staff photographer to use her darkroom to develop the film. If the climbers' excited descriptions were true, the pictures would reveal fabulous artifacts.

They watched as the picture began to take form in the developing solution. When distinct forms appeared, they realized what they were seeing. Row after row of clay pots and figurines lined both sides of a wide pathway. The ceiling sparkled with clear stalactites. The icicle-like features were not damaged as in many caves Scarlet had seen. It appeared no one had set foot in the passage in a very long time. She could see bare footprints preserved in the dust. Glad Amber had instructed the climbers to not go beyond the edge, she hurried to the phone.

Though certain her boss was asleep, she did not hesitate to call him with the news. Whether the artifacts were 150 years old or a thousand years old, it was an amazing find.

The next call went to Amber. When Amber first picked up the phone, she could hear Tammy instructing her technician to make more copies. When Tammy turned to the phone she said, "Get ready to do some exploring, this find is magnificent."

The agreement with *National Geographic* required Amber, Ray, and Don to be the first to explore new finds. *National Geographic* and the paper would report, document, and complete additional exploration.

Amber's diary entry: "This is almost too good to be true. How can I do something really good to help others feel like this? … gifts for climbers … gift for Tammy … something for the divers"

33

When they cleared away the tons of stone from the main passage, it was dumped in a series of piles nearly ten feet high. It rained, and the artifacts began to show as the dust and dirt was washed away.

With most the debris removed from the main passage, breakdown still covered what could possibly be a side passage. It could have been obscured for centuries. The cave was beginning to slowly reveal its secrets.

Amber called another meeting. She and the other Tridents, as they had begun calling each other, asked Britney to take them to an ice cream shop to eat and make some plans. Amber had paid a few thousand dollars to get some of the work done, and *National Geographic* had sprung for everything else.

Amber said, "How can we make some money?"

Don said, "We already have the gold. We have lots of money."

"I mean how can we make money from the cave? Many people and groups want to explore, excavate, or dig in the cave. Should we charge them a fee?"

Ray said, "If we charge the people or businesses that profit, then maybe we could let people who want to learn, or just look, come for free."

They agreed first priority was to maintain control of the entire operation and not lose any historical information. Based on the pictures of the upper passage, Amber thought a museum would be a good idea. Don offered to contact a museum curator and determine how museums made money. Ray brought up the subject of security. They were beginning to find things with high value on the black market.

Ray said, "If we are going to build a museum anyway, let's build it just inside the cave. Then we could have people enter through the museum. Small equipment could pass through a steel gate by the museum."

Don said, "Maybe we could build it out of the rocks we cleared out of the main passage. Then it would look natural."

Amber said, "To get the rocks cleaned and ready to reuse, we could allow kids and local adults to sift through the dirt while they clean the rocks. I could pay them, or they might want to do it for fun, or we could let them have a percent of what they find. Surely the pottery shards and arrowheads we are seeing are worth something."

* * *

Amber called a local stonemason who came out and made some sketches. He advised her to get a general contractor and that digging a foundation would likely unearth more artifacts.

Ray and Don marked off where they thought the museum should be with stakes. Mr. Spark asked a friend who was a general contractor for a quote based on the sketches. After a week, he came back with a plan for the museum, water and electricity, and an outside restroom. Using the stone already there, he estimated he could do the job using the local stone mason for $26,000.

At Amber's request, Scarlet contacted the University of Tennessee and talked to them about sending archeology students to do a "summer dig." They were excited to comply. A big job had finished, and they had a crew with nothing to do. Within two days, the students streamed in. They had loads of screens, shovels, wood stakes, buckets, and bags.

The grid was laid out along the foundation for the museum. They had done an initial estimate of depth by driving steel rods in the dirt and hit solid rock at three feet. Work began immediately. Amber suggested the students help supervise the local volunteers in sorting and searching for artifacts. She made sure to get all their names so they could be listed as volunteers and be given credit in the museum.

The boys thought it would be fair if one-third of the relics were divided between the screeners based on hours they had worked. An assembly line was arranged, and the process began. About fifty volunteers showed up the first day. Sifting screens and wheelbarrows were everywhere. No one was allowed in the cave. Word of the incredible finds had spread, and everyone was eager to see the relics. A display case with a Polaroid camera was put in the mouth of the cave. Whenever somebody found something, whether it was an arrowhead, a bead, or a pot shard, they got their picture taken with it before the artifact went into the case.

Water from the river was used to wash the screenings. The rocks were piled by size near the cave. As the display case filled, people of all ages came. Everyone wanted to be a part. Word spread, and people came from all around to help. Lots of onlookers came and went. A few people had to be asked to leave because they were loitering. It was difficult to manage the crowd. Someone tried to slip into the cave almost every day.

Ray, Don, and Amber worked when they were not supervising.

When Amber spotted something in her screen, she would let a smaller kid take over and go help someone else. The find went to the little kid or the other person. Amber wanted as many people as possible to be successful.

After a few days, the pile was reduced to the larger rocks. Ben had a friend with a backhoe come over to dig out the huge rocks so the sifters could keep working. Within a week, they were finished. The case was full of rocks, teeth, claws, arrowheads, hundreds of pot shards, spear points, tiny bowls, bone fishing hooks, pocket change, and a small gold nugget. There were also some sparkly stones and shiny river rocks. No one knew how many thousands of years people had inhabited the cave. It was a perfect location: dry, near woodlands, and near a river. The variations in certain types of artifacts suggested inhabitants over a large span of time.

The lead archeologist said, "An archeological dig, if done correctly, takes a lot of time and patience. Every square inch is tediously scraped and brushed to reveal bits of charcoal, bone, or even a pebble."

Amber was patient, but she was not sure she could afford to move at such a slow pace.

As they started with three four-foot grids separated by two four-foot balks. They found layers and signs of inhabitance. Different types of dirt indicated where walls had been and where cooking had occurred.

Amber watched them work for a few days and the progress was glacial. When asked what it would take to speed the process, they replied, "More people." To finish the three pits they had started might take another month.

Amber called Frank for advice on financing the museum. He asked if she had considered a career in public relations. "It seems your idea to have the public clean the rocks and sift for artifacts was a big success. Pictures of people holding their finds are all over town. I understand some of the better ones will be in the museum with the names of the amateur archaeologist who found them."

"It was Ray's idea," said Amber. "On another subject, I need your wise counsel."

"It's what you pay me for."

"I am trying to get the cave to start paying its own way. Once the museum is open, we can charge a small fee and make a little money. To build it, I need to spend thirty thousand dollars for a stone structure. Do you have any ideas for how we can make money in the meantime?"

"I have seen pictures of some of the artifacts in the upper cave. Have you considered selling or leasing some of them to famous museums?"

She said, "Are you kidding? Museums will pay to display some of the artifacts?"

"Yes, I believe so. I am surprised you have not been contacted yet. Talk with Scarlet about it."

Scarlet contacted several museums and supplied pictures and the history of the cave. Within a week, they were asking to see the artifacts and making offers to display the items in their museums.

Amber talked to Scarlet about displaying the artifacts in the cave. The passage was the perfect place, but it was only accessible from the "Sacrificial Pit". No one had explored past the room they were calling the "Sacrifice Room."

Ray and Don argued there had to be an easy passage to the area. They thought a place where many people came to worship or make sacrifices would have easier access.

34

They planned an expedition to see where the upper passage led. The first rule was to walk in single file to preserve the ancient footprints. Ray asked Tammy to join the expedition since she had been a photographer before she became a reporter. Even though she was scared of caves, she agreed to document the adventure on film.

By then, the Skeleton Passage had been cleared of bones. Some tight spots in the passage had been chipped away to keep people from getting stuck. Ray was the biggest one in the expedition, and he had been through the Skeleton Passage. They had learned to dress in tight layers to avoid snagging. Their small army surplus packs held plenty supplies. Amber packed an extra camera, flashbulbs, and film. She and Tammy brought notebooks.

The trip began with no fanfare. As Tammy took a few pictures of Amber, Ray, and Don, she said, "I see you all have matching necklaces, what is the story?"

Amber said, "I guess there is no secret now, let's show Tammy Ray's handiwork."

They each moved in close and clicked the three brass coin pieces into a single circular figure. As they looked up from the three piece puzzle, Tammy captured the moment. Assembled, there was enough definition of the original coin to make out the figure and the date.

Getting a picture of the four of them was more difficult. Tammy got them in close and took it with the big flash camera in one hand.

Tammy was apprehensive in the Skeleton Passage, but there was never a problem because she was small. After encouragement from all and clearing the tight squeeze, her confidence soared. She had to be slowed down more than once. Ray reminded her of the danger of a misstep and an injury.

Don and Ray alternated the lead. Tammy took lots of pictures of interesting features and posed in front of important areas like the water's edge and the "Sacrificial Pit". She got a picture of the message Amber had written in the dirt.

They went up the ladder, encouraging each other, with Don in the lead. At the top, the little group stood in awe. They could not see it all at once. It was like a warehouse. Jars and bowls of all shapes and sizes lined the walls for a hundred feet on each side. The scent of spices permeated the room. The ceiling was lined with translucent stalactites. Some jars were no bigger than a thumb.

Scarlet had been trying to get experts to help with dating the artifacts from looking at the pictures. Amber looked forward to a time when experts could see the artifacts like they viewed them now. After Tammy was finished with pictures and a couple of group shots with the artifacts, they moved on in single file. The footprints in the dust were various sizes, but none were very big.

Ray said, "Why are only children footprints in here?

Tammy took a photograph of Rays boot next to a tiny footprint.

Don said, "Maybe they were just small people."

Amber was drawing on her pad and writing down dimensions, and she fell behind. Tammy turned and took a photograph of her. With her back to the artifacts, she was haloed by stalactites. With a flashlight between her shoulder and cheek, her auburn hair was illuminated by the reflection of her notepad. Tammy made some adjustments to her camera and took another picture.

Ray called to the group, "Hey everyone, come look what I found."

The passage narrowed and began to curve and slope downhill. There were steps dug into the hard-packed dirt. Each step was capped with a flat rock. The rocks were different thicknesses, but the top surfaces were about the same.

Amber sketched quickly, and Tammy took pictures with and without people on the steps. They went across the entire passage. Ray and Don discussed the oddity of steps so wide on a path so narrow. Four people could stand easily on each landing.

Don said, "We told them when to expect us. Let's get on with the exploration."

Amber lagged behind again, keeping her map current. According to her compass, they were heading back toward the main cave. Though the steps had dropped them down ten feet, she believed they were still thirty feet above the main passage floor.

It was Don's turn to make a discovery. Beautiful flowstones and stalactites were all around the room. Their flashlights reflected off the wet surfaces. Thin formations, called soda straws, connected wet-topped surfaces with water in shallow puddles below. The water made the room feel especially humid, but it smelled clean. There was no stream carrying the water away. It just disappeared into the floor. The path curved through the features, but none of the beautiful formations seemed to have been damaged.

In the middle of the room, a large stalactite was suspended high above the center of a pool. In the middle of the pool, a stalagmite rose about three feet above the water. There was a gap of about three inches between the formations.

Tammy raised her camera to take a picture and lowered it back down. There was an odd lump near the top of the stalagmite. The color was different. In places, the surface was smooth like pottery. As she circled the pool and took pictures, she said, "A colorful ceramic jar was placed on top of the stalagmite to catch the drips of water from the stalactite above. Over the years or centuries, the jar became part of the stalagmite."

Amber said, "The layers of calcite could help determine when it was placed there. I've been reading about mammoth cave and some of the formations."

There were some crude benches fashioned from the native stone and formations near the path. Amber said, "Lunchtime, let's take a break."

They ate, drank, and changed batteries. Amber ate one last candy bar and announced it was time to explore. Don estimated they could explore another thirty minutes and still get out on time.

Amber took the lead. She was going slowly, mapping, counting her paces, and walking in straight lines where possible. As she was sketching, she stopped suddenly and looked around.

"What is it?" asked Tammy as she bumped into Amber.

"I am not sure. Give me a minute." Amber concentrated.

Everyone was quiet. A drop of water hit a puddle. Amber turned toward the sound. There was a dome in the ceiling thirty feet overhead. A group of long, tapered stalactites hung down. The longest one was directly over the stubby stalagmite that had caught Amber's attention.

A gold nugget sat atop the stalagmite on what looked like a solitary ring setting of stone. A few inches down, a pool of water trickled down the stalagmite. The bird egg-sized gold nugget was as shiny as the gold bars. Lumpy and imperfect, it looked like it had been deliberately placed to interact with the falling drops. Amber wondered about the source of the gold nugget. She had heard of no gold mines in Tennessee!

Tammy took pictures of Amber posing by the formation with her hand near the nugget.

Ray walked ahead a few paces beyond the room. A scream and a strained "help" came from the direction he had disappeared. Everyone ran in that direction as they heard Ray say, "There is a hole in the floor. Help me, hurry."

As Amber rounded the corner she looked down to see a Ray's fingers slipping from the edge of a pit in the floor. Dropping to her belly she reached over the ledge and grabbed for his arms just as he slipped.

Catching one arm she grabbed again and caught a hand full of hair with the other.

Don was soon alongside and grabbed his wrist. Tammy was focused her camera and took a picture before she took Ray's other wrist. Together they hauled him up and over the ledge. They ended in a pile beside the pit, trying to get their breath in the dark.

Don said. "What happened?"

"I turned the corner and was looking up at the formations. When I felt my foot slip on the edge, I was barely able to catch the rim as I went down. I was afraid you would run around the corner and fall in too. Thanks for pulling me out, even if it was by the hair."

Don handed Ray a spare flashlight. "I think we just leave yours down there for now."

Amber stood and assessed the situation. "This pit is about 8 feet across and a good twenty feet deep. We would need a ladder laid across it to get to the other side."

Turning to her right she said. "The passage goes on in that direction too."

Don said, "That will have to wait for another trip. As soon as Ray is able we need to start back to stay on schedule. Tammy, want to lead the way?"

Amber smiled seeing Don begin to take on more leadership responsibilities. He generally expected Amber and Ray to make almost all the decisions. She also realized Don was being fair to Tammy—helping her feel like she was part of the team.

Tammy was ahead of the others, and stopped suddenly. Amber came along side and followed her gaze. Amber said, "Tammy is about to teach us an important cave explorer lesson. Since our lights only cover a small part of our surroundings going in, cavers often find things on the way out that they missed completely. It's also why they often stop and look back to make sure they will recognize the way out. Tammy, show us what we walked right past."

As the four lights shined on the angled wall above the smaller passage, no one could speak. It was unclear whether it was a map, a mural, or a story, but it was definitely art. Mixed reds, oranges, blacks, and grays covered the flat face. It was like a billboard over a tunnel.

Tammy remembered the camera and took a distant shot and several closer shots. As she panned across the painting, all sorts of figures were represented. Many styles of figures were used. It was as if the painting had been added to until almost every inch had some type of figure.

Once the click of the camera broke the silence, they all talked at once and patted Tammy on the back. Amber gave her a hug and took the camera. "Stand below in the passage. I want a picture of you and your discovery. How do you like the sound of Tammy's Tapestry?"

Don insisted they go to the Sacrificial Chamber and rest before climbing down the ladder. While there, they ate and drank again.

Amber selected a flask-sized bottle from the wall. It was colored with browns and reds and turquoise. It was not perfectly shaped, but it was beautiful.

Tammy was quick with the camera and snapped a picture as Amber lifted the flask. She took another as Amber began to pull the ceramic cork from the bottle.

Ray said, "Amber, wait. We don't know if anything is in there—and what it might be. How about we take it with us and have it opened in a lab or a controlled environment? Does it feel like it has anything inside?"

She shook it gently and then a little harder. "Something is in there." She couldn't tell for sure if it was liquid. The top looked like it had something like glue around it. "Maybe it was sealed with wax." She wrapped it in a cloth and packed it away. The remainder of the trip out was almost boring after all the discoveries.

Tammy could not wait to get to the dark room and make a call. Scarlet lived in Nashville, but she worked with *National Geographic* teams from all over the world. She was more than willing to make the two-hour drive to see the latest discoveries. She also needed to fill the team in on some museum offers.

Amber ate supper while Ray and Don went home with big stories of adventure for Ben and Britney. Amber called Preston to fill him in on the day's events.

Amber said, "What do you think about me building a small museum just inside the cave. I have famous museums offering to pay me to display artifacts. With that money, I can have free admission."

"That is a wonderful idea. I am so proud of you. In Just a few weeks, you have gotten more out of the old farm than I did in a lifetime. You know your father would have been proud of you too. He always wanted to make something out of that old cave. I guess it was meant for you to make his dreams come true.

I have been getting reports on you too. I love how you are giving to others. Frank says most times you try to do it quietly but he still hears about it. You keep treating people well and it won't go un-rewarded."

Amber's diary entry: "Like a dream world ... those tiny footprints ... like his"

*   *   *

Tammy called the next day and wanted to show the photos to everyone.

Amber suggested inviting the sheriff, Frank, Ben, and Britney. Scarlet was already on her way down from Nashville. Tammy and her photographer had spent most of the night making eight-by-tens of all the good shots.

They cleared a path for the sheriff as he brought in three boxes of pizza. Amber had iced tea on the table. The pictures were fabulous. They really needed an anthropologist, an archaeologist, and someone who knew the history of the Native Americans and their ancestors.

Amber presented the small bottle and said, "Anyone want some sauce on your pizza?"

They laughed and decided it would be better if the bottle were tested in a lab first. They did note the color was fired in the clay and not painted on. The patterns on the little flask were engraved.

Don looked at the bottom, hoping to find a mark, but he saw nothing of interest.

Pushing a picture of the steps in the cave to the center of the table, Ray asked, "Why do you think those steps were there? There were other slopes with no steps. These were the only ones in the passage."

Amber waited until everyone had an opportunity to speak before saying, "Maybe we have to change our point of view." She shuffled through the pictures until she found more pictures taken around the steps. "Here is one looking back at the steps. It looks like a tiny amphitheater. Are they risers or seats?" She thumbed through the pictures again and selected one taken near the big pool. "See these little benches? The top is thin rocks like the steps."

The sheriff said, "You know, Amber, we could use a detective like you in the sheriff's office. Good thinking."

They decided to do a sound check when they went back to see if the steps were for a choir or maybe to listen to a speaker.

The sheriff asked, "Did someone find a bit of gold?"

"Yes, we still have it," replied Amber.

The sheriff said, "I would not want to disturb the nugget on the stalagmite, but it would be interesting to see if the two nuggets tested the same. I wonder if they were traded with someone from another area. I know researchers are interested in how societies traded. If you still have the collection of shiny rocks, you might have a gemologist have a look at them. There is a gem show in Huntsville next weekend. Maybe you should have someone take at them down there."

Scarlet said, "Tammy, these pictures are excellent. Would you be willing to contribute some pictures and commentary if we can update our story before it goes out?"

Tammy was flattered and almost said yes before consulting Amber.

Amber said, "With the gates in place, we are fairly secure now. I think it would be great for everyone. Ray, Don, what do you think?"

Two nods came quickly.

Scarlet pushed the pictures around and found one of Amber sketching in her notepad with the artifacts in the background. Translucent stalactites sparkled above. Her hair glowed like fire. A simple curved pendant glinted in the flash of the camera.

"Tammy, this is magazine-quality stuff."

Amber thought back to the fire. Her hair had burned off, and her body was covered in burns and bandages. She would never have thought her image would ever be in a national magazine. It was a wonderful picture of her, smudged with dirt, with priceless artifacts in the background. It was a fitting image of her sketching out what was ahead. She said, "I like it too, Tammy. Thanks for looking for the best and capturing the moment. You are good at seeing things like the painted wall. Everyone, we decided to call it Tammy's Tapestry. Maybe we will find that written on the wall in some ancient language."

Ray said, "Where did your sketch of the latest trip end on your cave map? Are we any closer to finding another way in?"

"We have three things to look for. One: The flat face of Tammy's Tapestry might have a matching rock face somewhere in the lower cave. Two: The water in the wet part of the cave has to go somewhere. Are there any areas in the lower cave with water or any springs coming out on the hillside? Three: If we continue following the main passage beyond where we explored, will it end in breakdown? I think it will."

"Why do you think so?" asked Ray.

Amber said, "The upper passage seems to have been a big part of life many years ago. Then, for perhaps centuries, no one has come in or gone out. I think the upper level was sealed off by an earthquake or a cave-in. It must have been substantial; otherwise, the inhabitants would have dug out or dug back in."

The sheriff said, "What else do you think? You seem to have good instincts about this stuff."

"Remember where we cleared the breakdown from the main cave and there was a place on the right side that I believed could someday be dug out more? I think that leads to the upper level."

35

The phone rang. A lady who claimed to be from Child Protective Services asked. "May I please speak with Amber Preston?"

"What is your name please?"

"Ms. Smith."

"What county are you working in?" asked Amber.

"Why are you asking all these questions?"

"I ask because a stranger has called me and is asking similar questions. If I am not satisfied you are from Child Services, I will end the conversation. If you have legitimate business with me, I will be glad to see you."

The woman identified herself more clearly—and her employer—and asked to come by to talk.

Amber suggested a lunchtime meeting, and the woman accepted.

When the woman arrived, the gate was open. Amber greeted her on the porch wearing her "Grillin Grandad" apron. As they shook hands,

Ms. Smith looked toward the river where a dozen cars and trucks were parked. "What is going on over there?"

"I had to put you off until lunchtime to get them settled and working this morning. About twenty-five college students and teachers are working for me in and around the cave. It takes a lot to keep them in supplies and all their questions answered."

A truck pulled in with a compressor and drilling equipment on a trailer. He stopped and waved at Amber. "Where do you want this?"

"Unload them past the cave—as close to the bluff as you can get," said Amber.

With a wave, he drove away.

Amber invited Ms. Smith into the kitchen as she hurried to pull a steaming casserole from the oven. She had the table set for four and as if on cue, Britney and Frank stepped in from the living room.

Mr. Frank introduced Britney Spark as a guardian and himself as Amber's Attorney.

Ms. Smith said, "This casserole is excellent."

Amber said, "Thank You, it's Australian."

Ms. Smith said, "We might as well get to the reason for my visit. A caller claimed that Miss Amber Preston, a fourteen-year-old minor, was living at this address with no adult supervision. The person insisted that I immediately check into this before something bad happened to her."

Britney said, "We appreciate the concern, but the report was inaccurate. My husband and I are keeping a close eye on Amber."

Ms. Smith asked, "And, Frank, what is your role in this?"

"I have a couple of roles actually. I helped write and execute papers dealing with Ms. Preston's guardianship and the transfer of property to her. Amber owns this 260-acre farm, the house, and the equipment. She manages the cave exploration and building the museum. She is the primary trustee of the artifacts and treasure found in the cave."

Amber said, "And I am anxiously awaiting the start of school so I can make some new friends. Meeting new friends and new teachers will be a real adventure."

"Well, unless you are putting on an elaborate hoax here, I would say there is no need for Child Protective Services to be concerned."

"Ms. Smith, are you by chance new to the area?" Frank asked.

"Yes, I have only been here a week actually. I am trying to get to all the referrals before school starts."

"I thought someone might be trying to take advantage of your unfamiliarity with the area and people in the community. Someone has been doing things lately to try to make life difficult for Amber. It would not surprise me to find this gentleman is the one who sent you out. However, my guess is he wanted to remain anonymous. Am I correct?"

"Yes, you are."

Frank slid a copy of *National Geographic* to Ms. Smith. On the cover was Amber's picture with the artifacts in the background. The headline for the main story was "Priceless Treasures Found by Young Adventurers in Tennessee."

After paging through the article, Ms. Smith said, "I think this case is closed. When we finish lunch, I need two things from you. May I have a copy of your recipe and a look at the cave activities?"

At the cave, the students were working as quickly as they could. They would soon be headed back to the university so everyone was trying to finish the remaining grids. The completed grids were four-foot square—three feet down to solid rock. Every bit of dirt and rock from the small pits had to be sifted for artifacts by an assembly line of students and volunteers. A labeled bag was poured into a coarse screen framework and gently rocked back and forth to allow smaller dirt and debris to fall through the screen.

Ms. Smith took a turn, and as most of the dirt slipped through the screen, some sticks and a perfect arrowhead remained on the wire. Oohs and aahs and words of congratulations came from everyone who saw the screen.

Amber held the artifact overhead. "Okay, who can identify this arrowhead?"

A sunburned freckle-faced lady stepped forward and took the point. She rolled it over in her palm and said, "It is a fluted Clovis point ... made between ten and thirteen thousand years ago. Nice find, lady."

Ms. Smith was hooked.

36

After Frank's detective contacted Amber's mom in Mexico, she waited a few days before calling Amber. Her latest lab results were due soon. She had gained five pounds and was hopeful she was making some progress.

The doctor told her she was not out of the woods, but she was beginning to show signs of improvement. He cautioned her that she still had more treatments, but he wanted her to take two weeks off the medication to let her body begin to rebuild.

Lisa called the farm, and Amber answered. After talking for an hour, the mother and daughter had salvaged the strained relationship. Amber asked if she could come to the farm. Arrangements were made, and Amber agreed to have her picked up in Nashville in two days.

Britney volunteered to drive Amber to get her mom. She expected her mom to look much better since she was getting out of the treatment center for two weeks, but she looked far worse. When they hugged,

Amber could feel her bones. She had put on makeup, and her face still looked pretty. Amber was about to comment on the scarf until she realized her mother was bald.

They talked for an hour as they drove home, and then Lisa fell asleep. Britney and Amber made plans. Her mom only had a week with her, and she wanted to make the best of it.

After a few days of rest, Lisa seemed to be better. She was amazed at all the activity. She spent most her time in the house since she could not risk infections or injury.

While Lisa was resting in the living room, she looked through Amber's album that documented the summer's adventures. As she looked through the huge photo album, Amber filled in all the details. It had been an extraordinary summer. When Lisa saw a picture taken the day Amber came out of the river, there was a familiar man in the photo.

"Amber, who is this man?"

At first, Amber didn't seem to know. Then it came to her. It was the man with the slicked-back hair who tried to poison the cattle!

"How do you know him?"

Lisa said, "He came to see me the day of the fire. He offered me money for Preston's farm if I got it in the will when Preston died. I told him to get lost and leave me alone. He got ugly and yelled at me before he left fuming mad."

Amber put together the puzzle pieces and called the sheriff. It was the same Victor Deal who had asked about buying the farm while the sheriff was at the house. Neither Amber nor the sheriff thought it was a coincidence that he was in Nashville on the night of the fire.

37

Rage flared in Amber. She left the house and went to the picnic table by the river to cool off. Thoughts swirled in her head. Her step father was accused of starting the fire. Now, here was someone else who could have done it. He could have put her through all that pain. He could have been responsible for …

Don said, "Hey Amber, your mom said you left upset, headed this direction. Since you are staring into the sky, you must have something on your mind." Flipping a coin her direction, he said, "A penny for your thoughts."

As Don lay on a bench staring skyward, Amber shared about Victor Deal and the probability he set the fire. She could not express how much it hurt to re-live the tragic night. The guilt she had kept deep inside threatened to come to the surface. Finally, she just cried quietly while

Don waited. Long minutes later, her tears dried by the hot summer night, Don walked her back to the house.

* * *

Victor Deal was so tired of seeing pictures and stories of the girl who had found his gold. Even with several big deals going around middle Tennessee, Victor had to have the cave. At first, it was the gold. The note from his ancestor told him it was in Preston's cave. Victor believed he had a right to the gold. If he had gotten the farm and cave as planned, he would have had it all: the publicity and the fame. Now some kid had it all!

* * *

Amber and the boys spent some time going over every picture in the big album. They were looking for something specific and paying special attention to any pictures of crowds or groups. Victor Deal was the target. He was the sheriff's top suspect.

They came across Amber's early pictures of the two scruffy men trying to steal the riding mower. A few minutes later, Amber found a picture of the same pickup truck parked at the back of the crowd, waiting to get onto the property, as the armored truck approached.

Don looked them over and said, "Wait a minute!" He pulled out several pictures: the scruffy men, their truck leaving the shed, the truck in the back of the crowd, and Victor Deal in the crowd. He started flipping through the albums. "I just remembered something." He pulled out a photo of a man leaning in the driver's side window and talking to someone. It was after they had the community come out to sift through the breakdown. There were lots of cars and pickups, but only one had a solid camper top. The man with the slicked-back hair was talking with the men who tried to steal the riding mower!

Amber looked over his shoulder and gave it a big squeeze. "Now who is the detective? We need to call the sheriff. Now we know they are working together."

When the sheriff showed up, he recognized the scruffy man in the pickup truck as the man who went up to the cave with the bleeding head. The sheriff said, "I will get pictures from Scarlet from the rescue."

Amber said, "I have a blood sample on a nail board in the shed if that will help."

The sheriff said, "Do I even want to know how you got that? I can see there is a competition for the detective job now. In fact, all of you are probably after my job. I'd better be on my toes." The sheriff took the pictures with him.

38

With only six weeks before school started, Ray wanted to find a connection to the upper passages. Amber's map was good, but it was not accurate like a real survey. He suggested getting a local guy to bring in a backhoe to drag out some of the rocks along the side where Amber thought there might be a passage. It was a bit risky, and they would need to be extra careful.

The friend parked outside the cave and shut down the backhoe. They all walked back with flashlights and discussed strategy. He suggested moving the rocks from the passage, piling them near the front, and then pushing them outside for screening later.

As he eased the backhoe into position, everyone stayed clear and watched for any signs of danger. He was making good headway until the rocks above the cleared area started sliding toward his bucket.

Shutting off the backhoe, they all went ahead cautiously to see how much more rock had fallen. At the top of the pile, there was a flat rock that was as big as a king-sized bed.

"Too big to pick up," he said. "But, with it on top of the pile, I might be able to dig to one side and make it slide out of the way."

The plan worked a little too well. When it slid, it did not stop easily. It hit the outrigger and knocked the backhoe to the side. They looked closely at the pile of rocks. There was a big gap where the rock had been. Ray climbed up the rubble, shined his light across the pile, and saw a small opening.

In the spot where the big rock had dropped from the ceiling above, there was an open hole to the upper passage.

Ray climbed down from the pile of rubble and went directly to the flat rock. He shined his flashlight across the top surface and let out a whoop! Everyone came over to look. There were tiny footprints in the dried dirt on top of the rock. The footprints were identical to those in the Sacrificial Chamber.

They spent another hour dragging rocks out of the opening. He scraped the sides to dislodge any loose rocks and bumped his bucket up into the new hole left by the fallen rock. He started hauling the rocks out and piling them where the original piles of breakdown had been.

*   *   *

Up the river and on the far bank, a man was watching it all with binoculars. He had been waiting for an opportunity to get some of his treasure back. This might be his chance. The No Trespassing signs were still posted, but he did not plan on getting caught. He had seen the pictures of the artifacts in what they called the "upper level." He intended to leave with some of them tonight.

At ten o'clock Victor arrived. He put his gear in the boat and used the electric trolling motor to go across and tie up near the cave. The riverbank kept the shallow boat out of sight. Dressed in black coveralls, he had a miner's light on a helmet, a rope, and two bags to carry the treasure.

Getting into the cave was easy. A ladder was propped against one wall, and he moved it over to the new opening. Only one large stone still lay nearby. He piled his gear on the rock and propped the extension ladder in place. Victor hauled his equipment up the ladder. At the top, there was a large passage. A smooth dirt trail led up a gentle slope toward the back of the cave. After about a hundred feet, the passage split.

He chose the left passage, but soon changed his mind, returned to the fork, and took the other one. At the next fork, both choices looked the same. He turned left and kept going. Forced to bend over, he was glad to have a hard hat. As he guided one hand along the wall, he knocked a rock loose, and it rolled onto the floor ahead of him. When it stopped rolling, a skull was staring back at him. He jerked upright and screamed. His hat hit the rock ceiling, breaking his light. Victor was in total darkness.

Finally, after a minute, he could see a faint green glow. It was the dial of his watch. Though tiny, it was all the light in his world. He began to panic, frantically feeling for the light. When he found his helmet, he put it back on. Searching in the dark, he found the skull. When his fingers went in the eyeholes, he jerked back. His heart was racing.

He finally found his light, but the bulb felt like it was broken off in the reflector. He remembered the candle and the lighter in his pocket. He lit the candle, and after a minute of appreciating the light, he checked out his headlamp. It was broken. Unsure how long the candle would last, he started walking. Soon, he was on smooth stone with no dirt. It looked familiar. He wondered if he had turned around in the passage and gone the wrong way. The candle was already shorter. His best bet would be to try to get out. He didn't know which way was out. His heart thumped in his chest as he began to panic. He started walking again. He knew if he was going out of the cave, he would pass the skeleton head and his broken light again. He did not see them. He turned around and went in the other direction, walking faster because his candle was getting low.

When his candle was gone, he used the lighter to light some paper and then his cloth bags. Nothing burned very well.

* * *

The next day, Amber had the boys and the backhoe operator over for breakfast. He was going to move some more rocks to see if the passage continued where Ray had seen an opening.

After breakfast, they went down to the cave to find the extension ladder propped up in the new passage. They saw the disturbed dirt on the rock.

Don walked down to the river and saw a boat tied to a tree. "Maybe someone is still in there. I think we've seen this boat before. It's the one in the pictures when we had the divers rescue the man in the skeleton passage."

Ray said, "Take the battery out or take a wire off in case he comes out."

Don disabled the little motor. "Now what should we do?"

Amber said, "He is probably lost or hurt. Otherwise, he would have been gone before daylight."

Ray said, "One of those guys attacked the diver and knocked him out. We better call the sheriff and get a search team out here. They may have been in there all night."

The sheriff arrived in ten minutes, and the rescue squad was close behind.

Amber said, "We have not even been up the ladder. All we know about the passage up there is it has the same tiny footprints as the upper level in the back of the cave."

The sheriff climbed the ladder, shined his light around, and came back down. "We are looking for one man. He wears a size-twelve shoe."

Ray said, "That is pretty good detective work, Sheriff."

He shined his light around near the base of the ladder and found a tennis shoe pattern like the ones he had seen in the path above. In the middle of the sole was a number twelve. The sheriff said, "Yep, a regular Sherlock Holmes."

The sheriff gave his handcuffs and a key to the rescue squad. "Be careful. He could be very dangerous, hurt, and/or hypothermic. Follow his tracks. There is only one guy."

Rescuers went to the first fork and saw the tracks. To the left, one set was coming, and one set was going. They knew he must have doubled back and taken the right passage since only one set of prints led in. After a few hundred feet, they found him. He was alive, but he was hypothermic and barely responsive. They gave him hot coffee and wrapped him in blankets. Hot packs were used on his neck and arms, and they got him to eat some soup. His speech was nonsense, but he was getting more mobile. Having heard about the diver who got clubbed with a flashlight, they cuffed him once he could stand up.

When told he was cuffed for trespassing, he continued to mumble that everything should be his. With some effort, he climbed down the ladder in cuffs.

The medic said, "A few more hours, and this would have turned out much differently."

The sheriff read Victor his rights and took him to the infirmary. They checked him over and pronounced him well enough to go to jail. The sheriff fed him a hot supper and told him his car had been towed to the impound lot.

Victor was fingerprinted and had his mug shot taken. He was

charged with trespassing and attempted theft, but he insisted the gold was his—and he had proof of it.

The sheriff sent a copy of the fingerprints to the Nashville detective who had worked the fire case at Amber's home. The detective wanted to speak with the prisoner about his whereabouts on the night of the fire.

The sheriff asked the detective to come as soon as possible because he could not hold him long on a trespassing charge. It was just a matter of time before he called for his lawyer.

Amber called the sheriff and inquired about the prisoner. After learning the detective would interrogate him the next day, she felt some relief. Amber said, "I want to talk to him. If he murdered my ...'"

"Hold on Amber. Allow the detective do his job. You need to keep your distance and be careful what you say and do. Let the courts handle this."

The following morning, Victor was again reminded that he could have a lawyer.

Victor said, "The gold is mine. I have papers to prove it. My great great uncle wrote about the gold and where it was located. It was his and I am the rightful heir to all of it.

The detective asked, "Why did you set fire to Lisa Butler's home?"

Victor looked confused and said nothing.

"Why did you engage the services of the Crum brothers to break into the cave and steal the gold?"

"I did not hire them. They did it on their own."

"And is the gold the reason you poured strychnine into the water trough two years ago to try to kill Preston's cattle?"

He looked stunned.

"You probably thought you wiped all your fingerprints off the bottle before you threw it out, didn't you?" He looked down at his ink-stained fingers from the fingerprint kit. "Do you have anything to say for yourself?"

"The gold is mine. Anything I did was to get back what was mine."

"So you did set the fire? Lisa said you were enraged when she would not agree to your plan. And you did try to poison the cattle—to reduce the value of the farm? And the Crum brothers say it was all your idea. You hired them."

"They tried to double-cross me."

"How do you mean? They said they were working for you."

"They went a day early and were going to cut me out. Serves them right to get caught and get stuck in the cave."

"Like you were caught and stuck and arrested? I think they are ready to make a deal for reduced charges. I think you are done. So far, you have admitted to about half this stuff—and I know you did all of it. The sad thing is your great-uncle who wrote the letter was also a murderer and a liar. I have a letter from a soldier in the room on his deathbed swearing under God that your uncle stole some of the gold, shot and killed his commanding officer, and closed his fellow soldiers in the cave to die. Your great-uncle may have stolen a pocketful of gold, but he never owned any of it."

39

Tammy covered the story. Victor Deal admitted to everything: the fire, the poisoning, and the attempted theft. He was taken to Nashville to be prosecuted for arson and manslaughter. The Crum boys had not been seen.

Camped across the river from the cave, not far away, was a new green pickup truck. Two casually dressed, clean-shaven men sat around the campfire and enjoyed the late summer evening. One had a nasty scar across his head, but it was hidden by a cap. Both young men had a fever. It was gold fever. In their case, it was a fever for whatever they could steal from the cave.

Victor had been arrested, and all the attention was on him. The Crum brothers had a bold new plan. All their gear was ready—a small new boat and trolling motor, hard hats, miner's electric lights, ropes, batteries, food, and water—and they had sacks to carry out the treasure.

The bold part was taking a guide. The pretty little redhead could take them right to the treasure. At the right time, they would grab her and take their haul.

40

Amber called the rescue chief who had brought Victor out of the cave. She asked for details about their trip in the cave. She drew a sketch from their descriptions.

Since the start of summer, Amber, Ray, and Don had read up on cave exploring. They now had better gear and understood more about safety precautions. They asked Tammy to come along for pictures and the story. This time, Tammy had no hesitation; she was all in. They started with a posed picture of everyone in front of the big rock at the ladder.

Britney took a picture, wished them luck, and reminded them of the return time.

Many of the tiny footprints had been obliterated by Deal and the rescue team. They decided to follow the footprints and see where they led. At the fork, Amber stopped to draw the map. They went left. They came to a narrow section and slowed their pace. So far, they had only been in the cave for fifteen minutes. The walk was easy. The path was clear of rocks.

Ray was leading, and the group caught up to him. He looked at the walls, and something caught his eye.

Tammy captured the moment with her camera.

Ray pointed toward the carvings and painting on the wall. The solid white wall was shining with tiny crystals that looked like salt.

Don said, "That looks like gypsum."

Amber said, "What is gypsum? Is it valuable?"

"No, that's what dry wall is made of."

Ray said, "Look at the colors. It's not all white. If you back away you can see patterns."

Deep gouges formed complex shapes in the soft stone. In many places, the gouges were painted with deep red pigment. Other colors, like in the tapestry, flickered into view as they shined their lights around.

Tammy captured it all.

Ray, still in the lead, noticed something. He said, "Everyone, stand still and turn off your lights."

In a moment, Amber, Don, and Tammy saw it too. Light. A very dim light filtered into the room ahead. Ray eased forward with the lights off. After standing still in the dark for a while, their eyes adjusted to the dark.

A pale gray pyramid appeared. It was a shape in the dark. He looked up to see the source of the light. High in the ceiling, a thin beam of light barely affected the darkness. It was not enough to light the room, but it broke the darkness like dawn. The pyramid was a large pile of breakdown. It had been stacked and shaped into a stepped pyramid in the middle of the room. The stones were not cut or shaped; they were fitted together with dirt and smaller rocks. Tammy's camera flashed.

With lights on, they stepped into the large room, divided up, and circled the pyramid. Along the walls of the room, deep pockets or indentions had been carved into the side of the solid rock. Some of them were empty. Some were not!

Tammy was busy taking pictures. She had brought about a hundred flashbulbs and checked her pack to count her remaining bulbs. She said, "Amber, I hope you brought extra flash bulbs, I am already getting low."

Don moved around some of the containers. There were different sizes and different colors. Nothing was bright and shiny—only dull reds, browns, yellows and blues.

Amber told Don, "Pretend it's Christmas and pick through the containers. Shake them gently and find one that sounds interesting. We'll take it back and open it later to see what we have."

Most the containers seemed full, but they did not rattle or slosh. A larger one sounded like it had sticks in it and maybe gravel in the bottom. Too big to put in a pack, Don put it by the exit to get on the way out.

Amber looked at the pyramid and visualized an ancient path. "I am going to the top," she said as she nimbly picked her way up and around. There was a large flat rock at the top with leaves and debris that had fallen from the forest floor above. Checking for stability, she stood with her hands on her hips like a superhero. The camera flashed.

They took the other entrance through a meandering passage for another minute and came to a familiar split. To the left was the entrance to the wet passage with the stalagmites. To the right was the passage with the twenty-foot pit.

Ray and Don cheered their success while Amber gratefully connected the passages on her sketch. Having connected the front to the back of the cave, and run out of time, they decided to go back the way they had come through the Pyramid Room. Amber took a few minutes to detail her map. They stopped in the Pyramid Room for a break.

Before leaving the room, Ray suggested leaving a flashlight, some food, water, and supplies in a cubby. In case of an emergency a supply stash could come in handy. They all noted the location.

Don picked up the large amphora-like container as they left the Pyramid Room. Though they had now connected the Sacrificial Chamber with easy access to the front of the cave, more passages remained to be explored.

Tammy said, "Thank you so much for including me. I can't wait to develop these pictures." With hugs all around, she thanked Amber for the offer of dinner and sped away.

After a meal of left over casserole and peanut butter and jelly sandwiches, they all stared at the large ugly vase-shaped container Don had chosen to bring back. He had set it in the middle of the table like a giant centerpiece. The container had a different type seal than the small bottle they had opened before. It had a large ceramic plug with a raised tab to pull. However, the edges of the seal seemed to be hard like a resin. After the dishes were cleared away, they went outside to try to break the seal.

Don picked at the seal with his knife, and it chipped easily like varnish. He scraped around the seal and began to dig into a black hard tar-like substance. Amber took pictures. They tried heating the bottle, but it did not loosen.

Ray said, "Let's try to break the top and not the vase." After a short debate, he wrapped the neck of the vase with a towel and twisted it tightly. With the ball end of a small hammer, he tapped the plug near the center. With a second tap, the container split into pieces leaving Ray holding only a towel.

Breaking an artifact worth thousands of dollars would have horrified most adults, but Ray's shocked look was priceless. Don and Amber rolled in the grass laughing. Amber got a picture before Ray started laughing.

Ray said, "Usually my ideas work better than this."

Don said, "You should have seen the look on your face."

Once they focused on the contents in the grass, they became more serious. The gravel was more shiny stones. The sticks were bones and antlers, and some had stones embedded in the ends. They gathered all the sticks and stones and put them away. It was tedious but they managed to find everything in the grass. Even the tiny shards of pottery went in a box.

Amber put all the stones in a cloth sack and hid them. Not sure of their value, she was reluctant to put them in the display case with the sticks. The little bag held at least a pound of shiny rocks.

Amber said, "Well guys, at least we don't have to look around that big ugly vase on the kitchen table now."

Something about this find seemed important to Amber. Her mind went to work on the puzzle.

41

A small part of the passage to the upper level was still blocked with breakdown. The hole in the lower cave ceiling gave easy access using the ladder. Amber finished her map of the known cave and penciled in a curve connecting the breakdown a few feet away.

The kids spent a morning in the upper passage and explored the front of the cave. They found a few places where holes had been gouged into the rock wall to make a torch cavity. In one, they found a charred bundle of wood. A curious stone was embedded in the cave wall near two of these features. Though flush with the rock wall, it did not look natural.

Amber wiped the surface to reveal shiny black glass. Noting the location of the stones and torch holders on her map, she drew an uninterrupted straight line between two of the stones. She concluded that even though it was dark, inhabitants could move unobstructed from one torch to another just by walking toward the light.

After rubbing the dirt from the third black stone, Amber decided to try out a theory. With Ray holding a flashlight at one black stone, she walked past the next and looked back toward the black glass. She could see the flashlight even though she was around the corner. The glass pieces were mirrors that provided a step-by-step guide through the cave! Amber went to her sketch and worked out where the next mirror should be.

There was no mirror, but a small cavity had been carved into the cave wall. She scratched around directly below and found something. Wiping away the dust revealed an irregular-shaped piece of black glass that was the size of her hand. One side was perfectly flat and smooth, which meant the inhabitants of the cave had figured out a way to navigate the dark with one torch for the entire passage. The next piece fell in place in Amber's mind. She said, "What if the mirrors go all the way to the outside to daylight?"

At the front of the cave's upper level, near the ladder, Amber sketched a projected passage through the breakdown and penciled in a mirror. Then she drew a line out to the center of the entrance. The angle would provide light in daytime, and if they built a fire in the front, they would see firelight at night!

Looking over her shoulder Ray said, "Here we go again. She's on a roll. Don, you are going to love this."

They climbed down to the main passage near the front of the cave.

Amber walked around with her flashlight and drew an X in the dirt with her shoe. "I would build a fire here—barely inside where it does not rain and in the center of the opening to keep animals away and in line with the side passage to the upper level to reflect light."

Don said, "So X marks the spot?"

"Yep, I want to dig here."

Ray said, "And exactly what are we digging for?"

"If I had set up a mirror system, I would want a fire in the same place all the time. Then, even the smallest fire would still light the way to the back of the cave."

"So we are looking for a fire pit or some charred wood?" asked Don.

"Possibly, but I have a feeling it might be something else."

Ray said, "One thing I have learned this summer is to pay attention when you have one of those feelings."

Amber said, "Let's go to the house, get some lunch, and come back with some shovels."

Later, they piled dirt to the side to be screened. Some layers had charcoal and bits of gravel, but most of the dirt was free of large artifacts.

When they were two feet deep, Ray hit a rock.

Don took a turn, and the rock began to take form as they dug around it. When one side was exposed, it was about two feet high and four feet across. They continued to dig around the rock until it stood alone on a solid rock floor. It was roughly shaped but amazing. The stone had been carved like a large pedestal with a shallow dish top. Holes had been formed from the dish through the pedestal to a circular trough around the thick base.

They sat on the dirt embankment and admired their work.

Ray said, "We will be sore tomorrow. Now I know how a gravedigger feels."

Don said, "And I think it is worth it. I have never seen anything like this."

Amber said, "We need to get an expert to look at this. It may have more importance than light for the reflectors. Look at the notches around the top edge and the holes through the stone."

They left their shovels nearby and declared it a really good day.

Amber went home and called Scarlet and Tammy with the news. Tammy agreed to take some pictures and send some to Scarlet.

A quick trip to the library confirmed the black glass was likely obsidian. Frank was excited about the new discoveries. He was more convinced every day that this young lady was more special than anyone realized. Her perception was on another level. In fact, he guessed her IQ would be off the charts.

Amber redrew her sketch to show the path of light between each mirror, and she projected the position of the last mirror to the fire pit. She noticed the paths had been cleared in the passageways in direct lines with the mirrors. This confirmed that people had been guided by the reflectors in the dark. Amber made a note to check if any reflectors were near the pits in the back passages.

42

Amber was trying to wrap up a bunch of loose ends at the farm and finish some projects before school started. She wanted the cave secured even if only with temporary gates.

The next task was getting the museum curator tours completed and articles sent to the museums for testing. An archeologist was coming to look at the other artifacts they had in the china cabinets and the new fire pit.

While Ray and Don were shopping with Britney, Amber warmed up some tomato soup and relaxed. After a rest, she put on her boots and dressed to do some hard work.

She decided it was time to clean up around the cave. After all the work, there were piles of screens, wood stakes, and all manner of things that were out of place. Grabbing matches from the counter, she jogged to the cave.

Out in front in a clear area she gathered some sticks, paper, and cardboard and started a small fire. She thought about pulling up a chair and relaxing, but the junk needed to be cleaned up. Piling more debris on the fire, her thoughts subconsciously went back to the house fire. After staring into the fire for a while, she tamped the bad memories down and slowly regained a feeling of peace.

She stacked the screens behind the side passage breakdown. The ribbons and stakes went onto the fire. With a rake, she smoothed the dirt around the cave where it had been disturbed by all the work.

A small boat went down on the far side of the river, and she waved as people do at passing boats. With the mess cleaned up and the grounds in order, she sat by the crackling fire and watched the embers glow alternating red and black. By hard work and good fortune, she had grown past the immediate fear when she saw fire or smelled smoke. She had friends and adults who cared for her—and even hope that her mother might be in remission.

Amber realized she had resented her mother for leaving. Knowing why she left made it better. When she went back to Mexico for more treatment, she looked awful—but seemed to have more life in her eyes than when she arrived a week earlier. She promised to try to come back soon. As Amber pitched another stick in the fire, strong arms grabbed her from behind.

43

The clean-shaven and well-groomed Crum brothers had quietly motored back up the river by the bluff and tied up out of sight. The noise of the crackling fire masked their arrival. They dragged Amber kicking and squirming toward the cave. One of them held her and explained what they were going to do, and the other placed the ladder in the upper passage opening. They said they would not harm her if she cooperated.

One brother said with a sick grin, "If you give us any trouble, well, just use your imagination." He put on his helmet with a headlamp and slung his pack over a shoulder. "You can tell us all about the treasure while we take a hike together. We can use the map of the cave you put in the article. Now it will be easy to tell if you are trying to pull something over on us."

Amber decided it might have been a mistake to have provided such a detailed map, but then she realized there was no published map of the newly discovered entrance. Her thoughts were interrupted as they tied a rope around her waist.

"We got you on a short leash now. Don't try anything."

Harold Crum went up the ladder first. With Amber shoved against the ladder, he caught the rope thrown up by his brother. Pulling on the rope, he teased, "Come on up here, honey, and show us where the treasure is."

With a gouge from the Gerald below, she reluctantly climbed the ladder. The larger guy wisely stepped back since Amber was considering kicking him in the head on the way up. At the top, Harold wrapped the rope securely around his hand.

She couldn't pull free or try to run.

He pulled her ahead so his brother could get up and into the passage. "Now you get out in front and lead the way."

"Give me a light," said Amber.

"No, I don't think so," he said. "You might get away and run like a rabbit. You will have to do with the light I have and be careful of what's in your shadow."

Both men laughed as if that was really funny.

She started walking and thinking. No one knew where she was or when she would be back. The main clue was the fire and the ladder. If anyone came by, they might guess she was in here. They had a hard-and-fast rule that no one could go into the cave alone—ever!

Ray and Don were not expected to come over.

She began planning as she walked quickly and deliberately. She stepped over rocks without any break in her pace, hoping her captor might stumble. He did, but held tightly to the rope.

Then she remembered that Ray had stashed the food, water, and a spare flashlight in one of the cubbyholes. He had made it easy to find in the dim light of the room. Amber remembered him saying, "First cubbyhole at knee level. When you enter the room, you can feel for it easily."

They came to the fork in the passage, and without hesitation, she went left. Harold pulled back on the rope and said, "Whoa there, Missy. Let's stop and look at this map. I don't trust you."

She waited for him to realize his map was no good. She saw no reason to lead them the wrong way.

"Okay," he said. "Left is right."

"Are you sure?" asked Amber.

"Just go! We need to get the treasure and get out."

Amber was glad she had eaten the soup earlier in the day. She had a feeling her plan was going to take a lot of energy. She thought back to all the weeks of physical therapy: the weights, the stretching, and the running. She was faster than ever. She hoped she could outrun these guys if she ever got loose.

As they approached the Pyramid Room, she didn't bother to show them the wall carvings or the dim light in the ceiling. She simply went to the cubbyholes and pointed at some of the artifacts inside. She did not have much rope, and she had only a short time to find the flashlight and pocket it. While they were looking at artifacts, they would not be watching her. She slipped her hand along at knee level and felt the flashlight. Slipping it into her pocket, she moved ahead to be the tour guide. "What kind of treasure are you looking for? These clay pots are nice. I would say they are about ten thousand years old. These little ones would carry nicely, but you need to put some stuff between them to avoid breaking them. We have not found out what is in them yet because some people are concerned about the yellow fever."

They stopped. "What do you mean?"

"It's like the Black Plague that killed a quarter of the population of Europe in the 1600s. Or like the Spanish Flu that killed millions in 1918."

"You are trying to scare us." Without warning he took a medium-sized bottle and threw it onto a rock at the base of the pyramid. It shattered into pieces. No one spoke. Both men shined their lights on the shards. Thick black syrup dripped across the edge of the rock. Yellow foamy bubbles began to fizz as the black material oozed down. They both stepped back.

"What's the black stuff?" one of the Crum brothers asked.

"I don't know." Amber pulled tight against the rope as if she were scared. "Like I said, we have not been able to get it tested yet. The labs are afraid there might be smallpox or yellow fever."

"Why would there be a disease in a bottle?"

"No one knows. Apparently, they ran into this in the pyramids in Egypt. One theory is they used them like grenades and threw them into villages to spread disease."

Amber saw he was holding the rope loosely, and she reached as far out the rope toward him as she could. With the flashlight in her other hand, she snatched the rope from his hand and sprinted around the Pyramid Room.

It took them a few seconds to realize what had happened. They chased after her. Amber fumbled and got the flashlight turned on and tripped on a rock. Back on her feet, she ran toward the exit on the other side. They nearly caught up to her when she fell, so she ran even faster.

The Crum boys were in pretty good shape too. Amber had a plan, but it had to be executed perfectly. Staying just out of reach, she kept a little energy for a sudden burst of speed.

The passage leaving the Pyramid Room was winding but just above head height. She ran upright, but they had to lean over. Ahead, the left fork in the path went to the stalactite room and Tammy's Tapestry. No one had explored more than thirty feet to the right.

Taking the right turn at near full speed, they were almost able to reach the rope trailing behind her. Praying they kept focused on the rope; she accelerated the next three steps and leaped like an Olympic long jumper. She cleared the opening easily. Two loud thumps and groans—followed by screams and more thumps—let her know the Crum boys did not make the hurdle.

On their last trip, she and her friends did not have time to explore this section because there was a pit the width of the passage. It was about twenty feet deep and eight feet wide, and the sides were vertical. She had a feeling the two men were too banged up to get out. They hit the rock hard.

She eased over to the edge to take a look. Both were moaning on the hard rocks.

Tumbling to a stop on her side, the scrapes were eclipsed by a throbbing ankle. After crawling back to get her flashlight, she saw a helmet light near where she slid to a stop. Apparently one of their lights made it across but they did not. She stood and tested the ankle. She could walk and maybe run, but she could certainly not vault over the pit again. Kneeling at the edge of the pit, she asked, "How badly are you guys hurt?"

For a while, there was no answer. Then one of them said they both needed an ambulance quickly. After discussing their mutually bad situation, Amber decided to keep the headlamp as a spare and try to find another way out. Amber knew Ray and Don would eventually come looking, but she was not sure the Crum brothers would survive the wait.

With headlamp on and flashlight in her pocket, Amber limped into unexplored territory. At a split, she went right into a smaller passage. The tracks in the dirt and the carvings on the walls increased as she crawled forward. She felt comfort in seeing signs and handprints from ancient times—but trepidation that the tiny people might have fit where she could not pass.

The passage abruptly stopped. Perplexed, she backed up on her hands and knees, scanning all directions. A few feet back, she felt a slight air movement from above. The passage went up a few feet and continued in the same direction. She saw more handprints and pictures on the walls but the passage got smaller. Like in the skeleton passage, she crawled on her belly with arms extended and pushed the lights ahead. Rather than causing fear, the memory gave her courage.

A small bottle and a tiny figurine were in the passage, and she pushed them ahead with the lights. As she realized something felt different about her surroundings, she saw a familiar form ahead. She exited a hole in the wall onto a tiny rock shelf facing the pyramid.

She was about fifteen feet up the wall, too far to drop even with a good ankle. On her belly, she leaned over the edge. She could see more cubbyholes below her. She worked out a pattern of steps to direct her to the bottom safely. After slipping the jar and figurine into pockets and donning the headlamp, she turned and felt for the first foothold. She winced, but her injured ankle held strong. A minute later, she was down. Viewed from below, the passage looked much like the other cubbyholes.

She headed for the cave entrance and stopped at the stash for a candy bar and some water. As she neared the ladder to the lower level, she heard shouting.

Ray helped her down the ladder and scolded her about going into the cave alone.

Amber said, "We need to call the sheriff, ambulance, and rescue squad. The Crum brothers are back in the cave—and they're hurt badly."

Don said, "Can we leave them in there?

Ray said, "No, you're the one who's always concerned about stinking bodies in the cave. We wouldn't be able to go in for weeks if we left them inside."

Amber said, "Am I going to have to hobble to the house to call for help? They need a hospital."

Ray sprinted to Amber's house.

Don helped Amber limp over to the picnic table and said, "We were really worried about you. What happened?"

Amber asked, "Did you see a boat tied up on the river?"

"No."

"Take a look, I bet it's down there."

The boat was hidden beside the bluff.

Don and Ray returned to the picnic table at about the same time.

Ray said, "Tell us what happened."

By the time she finished a quick version, sirens were blaring in the distance. She pulled the figurine and the bottle from her pocket. Both were dirty and smudged from being in her sweaty pocket. Ray grabbed a water bottle and a rag from the cave, and Amber cleaned them. The little bottle was ornate, but the tiny figurine captured their attention. Both boys were in awe. The figure looked like Amber standing on the pyramid with her hands on her hips—it even had rusty red hair.

"Where did you find this?" asked Don.

Ray said, "The Pyramid Room?"

Amber nodded. "Remind me to tell you about my dream. The sheriff is almost here."

It took hours to get help to them with a ladder and stretchers. The sheriff told Amber she was beginning to cost the county a lot of money for rescues.

She said, "Not to mention the cost of housing all the prisoners."

"Well, it won't be so bad. Victor Deal is in Nashville and likely won't be coming back. These two guys will be in the hospital for a while."

"If you think getting all broken up will teach them a lesson, I will not press charges."

"After they kidnapped you, threatened you, forced you to lead them into the cave, and destroyed part of the artifacts, you would let them go?"

"I have been through a tough recovery like they will go through. They will have a lot of time to think. I might go talk to them in the hospital to see if they have had a change of heart."

44

On a scorching Saturday morning, Amber decided she wanted to see the Indian mound. The boys had mentioned it more than once, but she had never seen it. Since finding the fire pit, she wondered if there was any relation to the nearby Indian mound. Amber had read about Indian mounds in the library, but all the ones pictured were in open fields. She guessed that hundreds of years ago, her mound probably had no trees. Some were supposed to have been ceremonial mounds, and others were said to be raised platforms for villages.

Since spending so much of the summer with Ray and Don, Amber had adopted their habit of carrying a knife and often a walking stick. She grabbed her notebook and gear and headed out. Her ankle was back to normal, and she welcomed the exercise.

The river bordered the property and one edge of the woods. She set a course into the woods and headed straight for the center between the two creeks and the river.

Ducking under limbs and thick underbrush, she wished for an easier route. Something disappeared under some brush and was only visible for a second. Thinking it was likely a squirrel or a chipmunk, she kept walking. She saw the movement again. Four waddling skunks ducked in and out of the underbrush. Getting sprayed by skunks was not on her list of things to do today. She waited a few minutes to allow them to get clear of her path. Ray and Don had told her enough skunk stories to know she should stay clear especially if their tails were raised.

Continuing northwest, the trees changed, and the underbrush got thicker. Using her stick to part the brush she came to an area where the trees thinned to reveal a steep embankment. The trees thinned, and the land rose steeply in front of her. A well-worn path angled up the slope. Taking the easy trail, she wondered if deer kept this trail clear. At the top, she saw a clearing in the middle of the Indian mound. It looked like a little field or a garden. Something was growing in the garden.

Amber saw the dark green plants with the seven leaves fanned out, and knew she had stumbled upon something bad. She turned to go and heard some noise coming up the path she had just taken.

No one knew she was here—so it couldn't be Ray and Don. She dashed across the field, trying to get to the brush on the other side before whoever was coming got to the field. Glancing over her shoulder, she ducked down between the rows of marijuana plants, barely in time. After crawling to the end of a row, she ducked into the bushes. She peeked through the leaves and saw a tall man with a hat and a mustache looking straight in her direction.

To get further away, she started crawling toward Ray and Don's house. In the dense brush, she palmed her compass and set a course back toward her house using the trees for cover. Through a break in the trees, Amber could see an open field and her house in the distance. As she neared the house running at full speed, she heard a vehicle coming up the dirt road from the soybean fields near the river. The truck was owned by the family who leased the soybean land from Ben Spark. She had a sinking feeling that she knew who was in the truck.

Amber called the sheriff when she got home. By the time she changed her dirty clothes, brushed the sticks from her auburn curls, and got iced tea on the table, the sheriff had arrived.

After a calming sip of tea she said, "Have you ever been on the Indian mound?"

He said, "I went up there many years ago, and it's probably grown up in bushes since then."

Amber said, "You're correct. There are quite a few bushes there now. Who are the men who farm the soybean fields for Mr. Spark?"

"The Mason family."

Amber asked, "Aren't they the ones with a lot of influence in the county?"

"Well, the Masons farm most of the row crops in the county. They probably have the most money and influence of anyone around."

Amber nodded and explained. "I went to the mound today by myself. I found a small garden on the mound and it was marijuana. I heard someone coming so I hid and slipped away. Before I could get home a man in a white Mason Farm truck came from the Spark farm and saw me.

The sheriff said, "Did they come over here?"

"No, and the Masons—or their worker—could have innocently stumbled into the field of weed like I did."

The sheriff said, "I will find out. Stay clear of the mound and the Masons in the meantime."

In the afternoon, Ray and Don came over to tell Amber that their mom had invited them all to go to a movie later in the afternoon.

Amber asked the boys to take a short hike with her. "We are going back on the bluff where we rolled the boulder down. I want you to see something."

The bluff behind the cave was the highest point around. Amber chose an easy path that led gradually around the bluff to arrive at the top. They looked down over the farm and the river. It was summer, and everything was green.

Don pointed out the boulder by the gate and the tin roof of the sharecropper house in the woods.

Ray pointed and said, "There is the little clearing in the woods where you sneaked up on our camp that first night."

Don said, "Across the river you can see the clearing where the Crums camped out."

Amber asked Ray to describe the Indian mound.

He pointed to the woods and described how the mound was covered with small trees and bushes. He pointed to a darker area of the forest and said, "If you look really close, you can see a different color outline in the woods. The dark green is the Indian mound."

"Have you been there lately?" she asked.

"No. We probably haven't been there in a year or more," replied Don.

Amber and the boys sat down on some rocks. As they pitched some small rocks down the bluff, she said, "I got curious this morning and decided to see if I could find it. I guessed where it was and walked right to it. Someone has planted a crop on the mound. There are no trees."

Don asked, "Why would someone plant on your property?"

"What they planted is illegal. It's pot … marijuana."

Ray and Don thought she was kidding. They often pulled pranks and tricks on each other.

Amber assured them it was no prank—and she mentioned how she almost got caught by the man. "He saw me running across the field. I called the sheriff, but there is a problem. I think it's the Mason family."

"They rent the bean fields from Dad," said Ray.

"And almost everybody else in the county," said Don.

Amber said, "They have a lot of power and influence. If it is one or two of the boys, maybe nothing would happen. If they are doing this in other places in the county—and using their equipment and fertilize to cultivate the plants—they might have a big operation."

Don said, "And we might have a big problem."

Amber said, "I wanted you to know so you can stay away from the mound and the Masons until this is over. The sheriff said it is not unusual for people to grow illegal crops on other people's land so they can deny ownership. They usually choose an unoccupied farm or hunting land."

"What is the sheriff going to do?" asked Ray.

"He is going to try to catch them."

Don said, "Let's get to the movie. I don't want to miss this one. It's about some people on a lost island with dinosaurs."

45

A few days later, Amber talked to Ray about coming over and working on plans to build trails through the cave. She had big glasses of iced tea, her plans, and a large map of the cave on the picnic table.

She heard tires on gravel and thought Ray had ridden over with his mom. Amber recognized the truck and the mustache.

The man from the Indian mound swaggered up to the table and sat down across from her. Amber thought it would be a real good time for Ray to show up, especially if his mom or dad was driving.

He introduced himself as George and asked if she had heard of him.

She said, "No, not by name, but I know of the Mason family."

He said he knew who she was—and he thought it was time he got to know her better.

His demeanor changed. His face turned red, and he began gritting his teeth. He said, "Apparently, you have been saying things about the

Mason family. I can't let what you say lead to an embarrassing situation.
I have come here to convince you to keep your pretty little mouth shut.
The Masons are a very powerful family. The family gets whatever the
family wants." He picked up a glass of iced tea and drank deeply.

Amber said, "I would like you to leave now."

He said, "I bet you would—but you have not been taught a lesson
yet." He lunged across the table to grab her arms, but she had anticipated
his move. She pitched a glass of tea in his face and jumped away from
the table with the other glass in her hand.

He came over the table, but she ran toward the river and turned up
the path toward the sharecropper house. She spilled tea everywhere as
she ran, and when the glass was empty, she threw a line drive that hit
him square in the chest.

He staggered but kept running.

Amber turned on the speed. The only shelter nearby was the
sharecropper house. As she ran, she tried to plan how she could get
away or defend herself. He was almost twice her size and fit. She began
to scream as she ran. Not enough to slow her down, but to sound the
alarm, hoping he would stop and go back. She screamed more, but he
kept coming.

She took the same path as before and saw the house.

He was gaining on her.

Increasing her speed, she leaped onto the porch. The front door
was still open, and she dashed straight for the ladder. She was climbing
through the hole in the floor when he came into the room. His grab
barely missed her foot.

Amber was panting hard. The stink of whatever was dead made it
hard to breathe. Any second, he would be coming up the ladder. She
scrambled for something to defend herself. Grabbing a board like a
baseball bat, she focused on the top of the ladder.

George was not stupid. He knew sticking his head through the hole would be fatal. Putting his cap on a stick, he pushed it up through the hole.

Amber took the bait and crashed the board down on the hat, splintering the board against the floor.

Before Amber could find another board, he was coming up through the floor. His hand was guarding his grizzled face.

Amber kicked and screamed, holding to the bare rafters overhead. She held the rafters and kicked with all her might. After she landed a few solid blows to his head, he managed to grab her feet. She struggled, but his grip was like a vise. He climbed into the room holding her feet as she held the rafters and tried to kick free.

Lunging forward he grabbed her waist, and pulled her to the floor. As they hit the rotten floor, it collapsed beneath them. They crashed into the room below in a pile of splinters and dust. Though he was scratched and cut, Amber was still under him. The fall had nearly knocked her unconscious.

He sat on her legs and smiled viciously. "Now let's see what those scars look like." He grabbed the bottom of her T-shirt and started to pull it up.

Amber heard a metallic clang, and he fell to the side. Looking up through the dust and haze, she saw Ray's silly grin. He was holding the old metal pan. He said, "I couldn't let him see your scars. You said they were off-limits." Ray dragged the unconscious man off of Amber and helped her sit up. The back of her head was bleeding from a small puncture wound. He cut off part of his shirt and made her a headband. She had minor cuts and punctures all along her backside.

They removed George's boot strings to tie him up. Suddenly he sat up and grabbed both kids by their throats. Pushing them to the side, he rolled on top of them and pulled out a knife. At the sight of the knife, they stopped struggling. George reached over and picked up the loose boot strings. He ordered Amber to tie Ray's hands and feet. Then, still sitting on Amber's legs, he tied her and gagged them both. Tied together, they could not get up or move. George dusted off the debris, gave Amber a final kick, and went out of the house.

Amber and Ray were hurting but not badly injured. They felt lucky George had made his escape without hurting them worse.

Amber heard the crackle of fire and smelled smoke. Ray's eyes let her know he heard it too. The house was old and weathered and would burn like kindling. They had to get out. They tried to scream, but the filthy cloths were wadded in their mouths too tightly to get out.

Amber twisted toward Ray and put her face close to his. She was able to bite on a piece of his gag and pull it out. He did the same for her, and they could talk and scream.

George had taken Ray's knife, but he had not searched Amber. The fire was getting closer and hotter. It was in the room and climbing the walls. As the room filled with smoke, Amber closed her eyes and tried to keep out the horrible memories. She thought, *this cannot possibly be happening again.*

Ray was shouting over the sound of the fire. He reached for her with his bound hands and pawed at her pants.

She looked at him and began to understand his words: "Your knife. In your pocket."

Once they changed positions, he put his hand in her pocket and got the knife. He moved it up to her mouth, and she pulled the blade open with her teeth. Within seconds, he was cutting her hands free—and she freed him.

Flames were on all the walls, and the broken windows had fire licking out both sides. They crawled to the back door and pulled at the bottom. Slowly the door opened, and it was hanging by one hinge.

A cracking screech came from above, and the tin roof collapsed. They crawled out fast over the junk on the back porch and made it into the woods with only minor burns and some singed hair. They sat quietly in the woods in case George was waiting out front. They could not imagine him waiting around, but they could not take the chance. Within minutes, most of the house was gone. Once the walls caught inside and out, the flames were higher than the trees. The smoke rose in a gray and black cloud.

Don was at home when he saw the smoke. He shouted for his dad and ran at full speed toward the sharecropper house. He knew Ray and Amber were making plans for the cave, but this looked like a house fire.

As Ben drove to Amber's house, he saw a truck speeding out of the driveway. He recognized the truck and the driver. Taking the path toward the fire, he and Don arrived at the same time. They stood in front of the burning remnants of the house. The chimney was still standing, but the roof had fallen in—and the walls were nearly gone. They shouted for Amber and Ray.

Hearing their voices was like music. The roar and heat of the fire distorted the sound, but they knew they were safe. They walked around the house.

Don ran to meet them, and they hugged. Amber whimpered from the pain but Don didn't notice until he saw the blood. She was bleeding and they both had a few burns. Ben checked them over before everyone walked toward the house. Sirens shrieked in the distance.

The sheriff and an ambulance arrived at the same time. The paramedics cleaned and bandaged Amber's puncture wounds and attended to both their burns. Amber and Ray identified George, and Ben confirmed he had seen him leaving the farm in a truck.

The paramedics wanted to check her over more thoroughly, but Amber declined. She asked them to leave her a few bandages for later.

George was not a Mason, but he had grown up with the Mason boys. His only relative in the area was an uncle, Victor Deal.

The sheriff made sure he had everything he needed to make a case for arresting George Gomez, but by the time he went with his arrest warrant, George was nowhere to be found. Apparently, he had stolen one of the Masons' trucks and left town. The Masons knew nothing about the missing truck until the sheriff called looking for George. They also seemed to know nothing about the patch of marijuana and figured it must have been something George was doing on his own time. Since he had friends in Mexico, they expected he was headed somewhere with a beach south of the border. The Masons did not seem to be too worried about either George or the truck.

After the fire was burned out and cooled off, the sheriff, Amber, and boys looked over the sight. Amber picked up the pan, and it had an extra dent.

Ray kicked around in the ashes and came up with the remnants of Amber's pocketknife. He handed it to Amber. "Here is another souvenir for you."

Amber planned to add the pan and the pocketknife to her collection on the three-cornered shelf. Amber thanked Ray more than once for coming to her rescue. He credited Amber with leaving a trail of spilled tea to get him started in the right direction and for screaming to keep him on track. They agreed it took a team effort to get out of that one.

46

The name Trident Cave was beginning to be used after it appeared in a few articles. Many speculated about the origin of the name, but no one knew for sure. It was exactly as Tammy had hoped. Create a bit of mystique, something else unanswered to speculate and talk about. Though Amber, Don, and Ray liked the idea of being Tridents, they found themselves renamed by the community as "the Trio." Everyone knew they were a team. They lived next door and did almost everything together. Word was that they split the gold three ways, even-steven.

Frank had volunteered to drive the Trio to Huntsville, Alabama, for the gem show. They could talk to experts and meet a museum curator from Atlanta. Amber had a pouch in one pocket with the shiny stones and a small gold nugget in the other pocket. In a small handbag, she carried the little bottle.

Frank had a briefcase with copies of many of the close-up pictures of artifacts, including the tapestry, the gold nugget on the stalagmite, and the pottery embedded in the stalagmite.

They walked around and were amazed by the beauty and variety of stones. Most were cut and polished and ready for jewelry. Some, however, did not look much different than some of the shiny stones in Amber's pouch. They stopped at a large booth for "Harry's Sparkling Treasures," which was crowded with visitors. An older gentleman stood in the back, letting all the young people deal with the customers who were looking at their merchandise.

Amber walked to the back and introduced herself to the older gentleman. She asked if he was a gemologist. He confirmed he was Harry: the owner, a certified gemologist, and rock hound for many years. He was turning over most of his business to his kids and grandkids. He nodded toward the front of the booth.

Amber said, "Would you take a look at my bag of shiny rocks?"

He motioned for them to sit and said, "I believe I will never be too old to look at a bag of shiny rocks."

Introductions were made, but the old man hardly seemed to notice. He was already pouring the contents of the bag into a thin row on a black velvet cloth. He gently flattened the stones out with a finger and studied the collection for a moment.

Reaching under the small desk, he came up with a jeweler's loupe and a weathered wooden box. He took out some cloths, a bottle of fluid, and some tweezer-like tools. With the small blade, he systematically divided the stones by color and moved a number of stones over to the side. "These are, in fact, shiny rocks. Though very pretty, they can be found in pea gravel or a riverbed."

He looked more closely at the remaining dozen or so stones and made an occasional groan or sniffle as he examined the stones. Amber thought they might just be the sounds old men make. He divided the stones into even smaller groups. "Would you mind if I cleaned these stones a bit?"

Amber said, "No, of course not."

He bent down behind the desk, and like a magician, unveiled another old wooden box from beneath another black silk cloth. Then he brought up a small machine with a soft wheel on one side. After wiping a stone clean, he carefully polished the stone on the cloth wheel.

They hardly recognized the stone. It was much clearer and dazzling with tiny facets now visible. "May I ask where you got this stone, young lady? Not specifically of course. Just tell me the state."

"Tennessee … an hour from here."

He removed the loupe and handed the stone to her. "I don't doubt your word, but if it came from where you say, it must have been dropped there by someone else. The stone in your hand is a very valuable uncut diamond, and I know of no diamond finds in Tennessee, except in jewelry stores and on the hands of some beautiful ladies."

Amber said, "We found some other things that were not native to the area." She pulled the little gold nugget from her pocket and put it on the table.

"Yes," he said. "I believe you did. Seeing this reminds me of an article I read recently about a young lady, about your age, who came across some extraordinary finds. Could you be the same young lady?"

"I believe you will recall there were two other young men who were equal parts in the discovery. This is Don and Ray. Frank is our friend and attorney."

"So they are, indeed." Standing, he reached out to shake their hands. "Hello gentlemen. Just call me Harry. I suppose I was drawn by the bag of shiny rocks and failed to see the shining rock stars right in front of me. One would think, after all these years, I would have learned to look at the people before the shiny things. As I was saying, this is the best stone. I will clean up the others a bit. Four more are diamonds, two are yellow topaz, and five may be rubies. I say all this quietly because the walls have ears. Like with gold, the lure of diamonds and gems is too much for some people. I am pleased you have these three gentlemen to protect you."

Ray and Don grinned with pride.

Frank looked a bit concerned. He asked, "What would their value be as they are today … uncut?"

"It is difficult to say without further polishing and closer assessment. Some could be flawed; some could be off-color." He pulled out a tiny scale, weighed each stone, and made a note in his pad for each. "Average-quality stones would be worth maybe forty-four thousand."

Amber said, "It sounds like about what it will cost to set up the museum."

"Since I have all but turned this business over to the children, would you have a need for a consultant who would help in these matters on an ongoing basis? The idea of a museum seems like the kind of thing an old rock hound would be useful for. I would be glad to volunteer now and again if you have a need."

Frank shook his head. "Amber, I don't see how you do it. Almost everyone you contact wants to help—and many of them at no cost. You even have your lawyer doing it. You must be living right."

After setting a time for him to check out the site, Harry gave them one of his brochures and a business card.

Their next appointment was with an archaeologist. He had suggested meeting at a friend's booth. Behind gem-polishing equipment, he had reserved a small table and chairs for their meeting. When they arrived, he stood and greeted them eagerly. Even though he had come highly recommended, Frank had checked his background thoroughly. The man went to a table and placed some soft cloths in the center. After putting on white cotton gloves, he asked if they had brought the piece.

Amber removed a sock from her bag and slid the little hot sauce-sized bottle into her hand.

He carefully took the bottle and turned it skillfully. Always keeping it over the cloths, he examined every inch.

To lighten things up, Ray said, "Nowhere on the bottle does it say how many ounces it holds."

The scientist looked over his glasses and shook his head.

Ray's comment didn't get a laugh but at least the man started talking.

He began to name pigments, and commented on the grooves in the bottle, the stopper, and the wax. In the end, he had more questions than answers. "Where did it come from? Are there other articles of the same time period? Have the contents of similar bottles been analyzed?"

He had seen a shard with similar designs and materials but never an intact article. He was very impressed.

Don said, "You haven't seen anything yet."

Frank spread the photographs across the table.

Amber said later, "I really thought he was going to wet his pants. He could not speak for two or three minutes. He wanted to come back with us when we left the show."

At the end of the meeting, he decided to bring three people to view the site. They would take detailed pictures of three artifacts in the cave and these pieces could be removed and taken for study.

Frank asked him to bring documents to transfer valuable articles between parties like museums. They had one other gemologist assess the stones, and he made an offer.

Feeling an obligation to give Harry an opportunity to counter or match the offer, they went back to his booth. As they got close, Amber could see he was taking a nap.

A few people in the crowd seemed to look at her a little too long as she was approaching Harry's booth. She was wondering if something about her clothing was wrong or if she had a big stain on her shirt where a bandage was leaking. Before she could wake up Harry, a girl about her age came up to her and said, "I am Kimmy, and you are Amber Preston. I loved the article." She turned to her friends and said, "I told you it was her." She held Amber's hand and said, "And you are Ray—and you are Don." She seemed like she was in another world.

Amber pulled her in for a hug and said, "Thank you. I am glad you liked the article. You seem to know my great friends too. Why don't you and your friends meet us at the food court in thirty minutes, and we can talk more over a milkshake? We need to speak with someone now, but we will look for you there."

A small crowd had gathered, and Amber smiled and waved. It took Ray and Don a few minutes to follow. "The girls are pretty—and they know our names?"

All the commotion near his booth woke Harry.

Amber told him the other gemologist had made an offer on the stones. She wanted to give him the first opportunity to buy them if he was interested.

He took the stones out and noted the other fellow had cleaned and polished all of them. The rubies were excellent, the topaz—though not as valuable—were very nice. Looking back at his notes, he made some additions.

"The number I gave you before was an estimate based on average stones. I can now see some of these are excellent and will make beautiful pieces. I am guessing you got a similar number to my estimate as an offer. I am afraid the fellow might be trying to offer you a bit less than they are worth. I believe I have an idea. Since you are building a museum, why don't we do this? The stones are worth about sixty-five thousand dollars uncut. I will give you the forty thousand you need for the museum, and I will cut and mount an excellent example of each diamond, topaz, and ruby for you to have in the museum as your own.

Amber looked to Ray and Don for their opinion. They nodded. "That's a good deal!"

Frank read over the paperwork, filled out an inventory list with the carat weights and descriptions from Harry's notebook, and added the details of the transaction. They signed the paper and passed it to Amber. While she signed, Harry pulled out a checkbook, wrote a check for $40,000, and handed it to Amber. He said, "There is a pay phone on the wall. Would you call the bank and make sure the check is good?" Not wanting to appear suspicious, she glanced at Frank. He handed her a quarter. While she was gone, Harry winked knowingly at Frank.

Amber was back in a few minutes with an odd look on her face.

Harry said, "Well, Amber, what did the bank say?"

Amber said, "Before I even gave them an amount, they said the check was good. Then I told them the amount, and they still said it would have been good if it were ten times as much."

Don said, "Then I guess you are rich."

"Well, yes, I am. And I have a lot of money too. Being rich isn't about money. Being rich is what you all are doing right now: enjoying life with good friends. And today, you have made another friend, which makes you even richer."

As they walked toward the food court to meet her fan club, Amber said, "Things are really falling into place. The gemologist is coming and offering to help. The curator is coming to look at the pottery and will take some to evaluate. We are sending the bottle to have the contents evaluated in a lab. Scarlet has two other museums sending representatives to make offers on leasing some articles. We decided to sell the gemstones to get revenue to build the museum. It's been a pretty good week."

Amber's thoughts went back to the bag of stones she had hidden after Ray broke the large container. There were ten times as many stones. If they were all diamonds, she might need some investment advice.

The gemologist was right about the walls having ears. It did not take long for word about the precious gemstones to spread around the exposition. Not everyone at the event was there with honorable intentions.

Amber's diary entry: "Being rich is enjoying life with good friends."

47

The Smithsonian Institute corresponded directly with Frank to try to buy or lease some artifacts. They agreed to test one bottle before moving ahead with a purchase.

Amber worked with Frank and Scarlet to invite representatives from three museums to meet at the cave. They reviewed pictures, took the tour, and picked a variety of pieces. Amber marked the diagram with their selections.

Part of the agreement was that each piece would be analyzed at the museum's expense. All data was the property of Amber, and she had exclusive proprietary rights.

The Smithsonian responded first and sent a special container to ship the tiny bottle for testing. Tammy took pictures as it was crated and shipped away.

A week later, they got a call.

"Preliminary testing is complete. Wax sealed the stopper of a ceramic bottle. Specific material details will follow. The glaze is a combination we have not seen in this country. It must be novel to this country because it predates any known trade."

Amber said, "How old is it?"

The researcher said, "Carbon dating puts it at thirteen thousand years old."

"What was in the bottle?"

"Seeds. They look like a very early version of corn. Again, nothing like we have ever seen."

Amber said, "I was really hoping for diamonds."

The researcher said, "These may prove to be more valuable. The seeds may still germinate. Can you imagine planting them and having a prehistoric plant—perhaps one that has been extinct for ten thousand years?"

Amber thought about the seeds she had planted beside her house. Yes, she could imagine growing a prehistoric plant! "Well, what do we do next?"

"I have put the seeds in a dry, sealed environment—much like the bottle they were in—except we can see into this one."

"I hope you took lots of pictures."

"Yes, more than you could possibly need. I have two colleagues I would like to involve in the project if I may. One is for the bottle, and one is for the seeds. Do I have your permission to let them take a look?"

"Yes, you do—as long as we retain control of all the seeds. How many seeds did you find?"

"I have not really counted them. There are perhaps forty-five or fifty."

"Would you take the time now to get an accurate count?"

In a few minutes, he was back on the phone. "I really should have made a count earlier. I was so excited about the find that I did not follow exact procedure. There are sixty-two grains. A few appear damaged or cracked, but there are sixty-two. Why is the number important to you?"

"I want to make sure in case there turns out to be significance to the numbers of things we find in other containers. It might relate to whether people could count or add."

"Oh my, you are right again. I was thinking of only one thing, and you are dealing with a much broader exploration. I saw the pictures of the room. It is amazing."

Amber thanked him for his work and said she looked forward to his report.

He said he would call back if the two other experts had any additional information.

48

Harry showed up for lunch, and Amber brought the casserole to the table. Harry, the Spark family, and Amber sat around the table.

Harry kept looking toward the artifacts in the china cabinet.

Amber said, "Harry, I don't have ice in the glasses yet. Why don't you take a look at the artifacts while I finish the drinks?"

He hurried over to the cabinets and scanned the contents of every shelf. The stones were obviously of interest, but the potsherds and teeth fascinated Harry too. After a quick look, he made his way back to the table and joined the others. "Amber, do you have any idea the magnitude of what you possess? Discoveries like this are rare. I know of nothing like this in North America. Managed correctly, this could be a lifelong source of income. You could preserve artifacts that have never been seen by humans as we know ourselves today. Most people do not have a good concept of time and how we human critters fit in. I saw a few Clovis points on the shelf. If the relics from inside are anything near that old, it will be extraordinary. Don speculated that the upper cave entrance collapsed and has been blocked for centuries. He is right to think when one group leaves, a later group occupies and remodels. Most of the really old stuff gets broken or buried. *We* are the next occupying group. Though you are doing an excellent job, Amber, I believe you need a professional to help you develop a long-term plan. You need someone who loves history and has a good track record in the field. I would also recommend getting someone wealthy who is not inclined to rob you blind."

Don said, "Someone wealthy like you?"

"No, no. Dear me, no. You need someone like one of the big museum philanthropists. I might know someone who can help if he is back in the country. He is quite savvy and a great adventurer."

Amber looked at Ray and Don and said, "After dinner, maybe we can give this fellow a call. What country is he working in?"

"He is examining a newly discovered pyramid ruin in Egypt."

Ray said, "It is probably a lot bigger than the one in the Trident Cave."

"Yes, it probably is, but yours could be twice as old. Rex is also an expert on cave art and is an excellent businessman. He helped me a few years back, and I was able to retire quite comfortably and turn a thriving business over to my children."

After dessert and a few minutes to digest and talk, Amber brought Harry the phone.

49

After the call, Amber asked, "Is Gulliver his real name? Rex Gulliver?"

"Yes, he gets ribbed about it all the time, but he doesn't mind. He doesn't have to change his name to fit his occupation."

Ben said, "What is his occupation?"

"I think philanthropist, adventurer, and business consultant would be a good title if he had one."

"Well, what did he say?" asked Ray.

"He is back in Washington, which is where he sometimes lives. He has read stories about all of you and will be flying in tomorrow about lunchtime."

Don said, "It will take two hours to get here from Nashville after he lands. He might miss lunch."

"I would not count on it. He is very resourceful and might surprise you. I have waited too long already—may I get a closer look at the artifacts?"

Amber's Diary Entry, "Adventurers studying pyramids ... Gulliver's travels ... Surround yourself with great people."

*   *   *

The next day at noon, as everyone was waiting for the pizzas to arrive, a strange sound came from near the river by the cave. The treetops were blowing around as a helicopter rose up above the river in front of the cave. Hovering for a minute, the copter rotated a full circle and tipped toward the house. Flying just over the roof, it landed smoothly in the front yard—just as Frank drove up with the pizzas. The rotors slowed to a stop, and everyone went out to meet Rex. He stored his helmet, grabbed a duffel bag, and jumped out of the cockpit.

Harry made introductions as they walked to the house.

Everyone gathered around the table and weighed in on the pizzas. Conversation spanned the globe and time from Egypt to Australia and back to the Civil War. When the subject of the cave came up, Amber filled him in on the latest developments. Amber did not dwell on the latest encounter with George and the burned house, but Ray made sure Rex knew the details.

Harry said, "Since many of the artifacts were given to the locals who screened them, maybe some would like their stones assessed to see if they have value. Some kids might have the makings of a college fund. I went through the pictures and saw a few gemstones."

Everyone thought it was a great idea.

After lunch, the boys worked with Harry, and Amber showed Rex around. Rex saw the artifacts, the photographs, and the front of the cave.

He was spellbound by the raised fire pit and called it a monumental discovery.

Amber asked to talk privately for a while. After leading him to the picnic table, she said, "I am new at this, and I want to do things right. A few months ago, I was nearly burned to death in a house fire, and I worked and cried and stretched and exercised my way back among the living. Good people, nurses, physical therapist, doctors, my mother, the sheriff, the Sharps, and others helped me be part of something extraordinary. They carried me on their shoulders and helped me acquire money and possessions. I like the feeling of giving to others. I am concerned about losing everything, including the good feeling of giving it away and helping others. Can you help me?"

"What do you want?" he asked.

"What do you mean?"

"Name everything you want—and start with the big stuff."

"I want to keep my friends, my farm, and the cave and somehow get it to keep producing money so I can help people. I want to have adventures. Ray, Don, and I all love school, but you should see us together. We are a team and really complement each other. It would be great to have adventures and go to school."

"Where do you want to live?"

"I have not traveled … so maybe it would be good to see the world before I decide. Ray, Don, and I have discussed starting an adventure company, but we don't know exactly what that would look like."

"How smart are the three of you?"

"Don is probably the smartest in math. We are all A students and could probably keep A's even if we only took the tests. I guess we are pretty smart, but there's so much to learn. There are so many books to read."

"Harry says we need someone to run the cave operation and someone like you to advise us."

"He is right. You are sitting on the proverbial gold mine, but it is vulnerable right now. By the way, what did you do with the gold? Have you spent it yet?"

"I gave most of it away. I gave a third to Ray and a third to Don. We all found it together. No one has spent any yet. It's all in the bank. It really is piled up in the bank. They had a second unused vault, and they rented it to me. Turns out it was good public relations for the bank."

"The secret to success is learning how to best make money and best give it away. You are already on the right track. Let's get with the others and do the grand tour."

"Do you need boots or a flashlight?"

"Would I be much of an adventurer if I did not come prepared?"

Amber said, "I suppose you are ready for anything. Before we explore, let's take a walk to the house. I want to show you my flower garden." Beside the house—and reaching just beyond the roof—were two tropical trees.

Rex looked them over closely.

Amber said, "I found some seeds in a tiny bottle in the cave and planted two of them here three weeks ago. Do you think I have a green thumb?"

Looking at the tops of the trees, Rex said, "You have more than a green thumb. We better come back to this development later. This may change everything. Let me get my gear. I will meet you at the cave."

When they gathered by the cave a few minutes later, he strolled up in a classic 1930s explorer's khaki shirt, pants, tall boots, and even a pith helmet. He had a small backpack on one shoulder and a camera over the other.

Harry laughed and said, "You do know how to make an entrance."

Rex took off his pith helmet and put it on Amber's head. "Just kidding—this is a souvenir for you. It belonged to George Andrew Reisner when he excavated the pyramid of Menkaure in Egypt in the early 1900s." From his pack, he extracted a hardhat and a lamp with a battery pack.

Amber put the pith helmet on a shelf and thanked Rex. "Let's skip the lower cave and get straight to the good stuff." Amber led the way, and Rex was awestruck by the tiny footprints and the reflector concept.

50

As they approached the Pyramid Room, Ray pointed out the painted carvings in the soft gypsum walls.

Rex took lots of pictures and Don told him to save some bulbs for the good stuff. Rex said many caves had breakdown in the center of a big room like this where the rocks overhead had collapsed after the cavity formed underneath. He had never seen one restacked into a recognizable pyramid. It was not a stacked pyramid in the classic sense, but if their information was accurate, it could be one of the oldest.

Ray asked Amber to go back to the top of the flat rock and pose like a superhero again. She had done it before on a whim.

Amber said, "I would, but I seem to have left my pith helmet for climbing pyramids at the house. I do wonder though, if the breakdown was in a big pile in a round room, why not make a cone shape and not a four sided pyramid? Could it have to do with the light coming in through the top?"

"What did you say?" asked Rex.

"There is a hole in the top, a crack in the rock, letting in a tiny bit of light. Everyone, turn off your lights for a few minutes."

They turned off their lights, and the gray pyramid appeared as everyone's eyes adjusted to the darkness.

With their lights back on, Rex said, "Someone can do a doctoral thesis on the light in relation to the room. There's so much potential here."

After leaving the Pyramid Room, they came to the split. To the right, they saw the pit and quickly moved back to the left passage. Amber pointed out the golden nugget stalagmite, the ceramic bowl stalagmite, and Tammy's Tapestry.

Rex stopped.

Don said, "Pretty cool, huh?"

Rex did not answer.

Harry said, "This is one of his specialties: writing, pictures, and graphics."

Rex pulled a little book from his pack and fanned through the pictures. "Amber, this graphic wall will do all the things you said you wanted. Are there more like this?"

"Not much so far … it's like this was one of the few places they were allowed to write. There is one small passage beyond the pit leading to the Pyramid Room. It has writing on the wall. No one has pictures yet."

Rex directed his light to the right and left of the graphics wall above the passage. After a few minutes, he pointed out some small ledges on each side that were carved into the stone below the mural. He turned to the group and said, "Anyone know the purpose of these features?"

After a moment to give others a chance, Amber answered, "We were all so focused on the mural that we did not take the time to look around and see where the timbers were supported while the work was done. They must have worked like scaffolding."

Rex said, "Amber goes to the front of the class."

Ray said, "So you know, Mr. Rex, Amber knows most of the stuff without trying. It's like she already knows stuff, and getting near something makes her remember it."

Rex looked over at Amber and said, "Is that accurate?"

"Sometimes … it's like intuition. Stuff just comes to me."

Don said, "When she found the golden nugget on the stalagmite, she was not even looking. She was writing in her notes."

Amber said, "It is because I heard it."

Harry said, "That's pretty spooky too. I can hardly hear anything without this hearing aid, much less a piece of gold sitting on a rock." That got a good laugh, and Amber was glad the focus was on someone else for a while.

They moved on and took a few pictures of the steps.

Amber asked if anyone could sing, and Rex said he had been known to sing a few notes.

Don explained how they were trying to decide if the steps were for the choir to sing or for the students to sit while someone talked. Rex went to the steps and stood in the center. Everyone else spread out in front. He burst into a rousing rendition of "Rocky Top," which seemed quite appropriate. Everyone clapped, but the acoustics were nothing special.

The group gathered on the steps, and Rex began singing as he walked around in front of the steps. When he reached a certain spot, everyone said stop. Something changed in that one spot. The sound was twice as loud. Rex changed places with Don who and recited the Preamble to the Constitution. It was loud and bold and perfectly clear.

"Mystery solved," said Amber.

"Another of Amber's intuitions," said Ray. "She is the one who noticed the step construction and speculated about a different purpose."

Rex walked up to Ray and said, "You seem very proud of Amber's leadership and intuition. Some people would be jealous."

"Not me … I never had so much fun in my life. We all contribute. I like to brag on Amber. I also brag on Don since he's the smartest."

In the Sacrificial Chamber, Rex took some pictures, went to the sacrificial pit, and climbed down the ladder. He took a few steps down the side passage, and Ray walked down to the water with him.

While they were gone, Harry, Amber, and Don talked as they had snacks.

Don said, "I am exactly like Rex except about a foot shorter. Maybe when I get older, my hair will turn dark red like his and yours, Amber."

Amber and Harry laughed.

Harry said, "Don, you are right about one thing. You are a lot like Rex. You're both smart, strong, and in the middle of a big opportunity. For you, Amber, and Ray, it will shape the remainder of your life. If you three can manage egos and greed, you will someday be as well-known as Rex."

Don said, "If he's so well-known, why have I never heard of him?"

Harry said, "A fair point. When I was your age, I wrote my name on a big fuel tank with spray paint. It did no harm. The rusty tank needed some paint. A neighbor came by, and I thought he was admiring my writing. He simply said, 'Fools' names and fools' faces are often seen in public places.' Rex must adhere to that philosophy. He prefers to do good stuff and not toot his own horn. He is very well-known among those in his field and among philanthropists."

Ray and Rex came back up the ladder, and Rex said, "Is that all you got?"

It took Amber a second to realize he was joking.

As they ate their snacks, Rex said, "The pit is probably full of historical data. A small excavation was done about a foot down. I will bet a thorough dig will yield a treasure trove of information."

Amber said, "I dreamed that little ladies were pouring stuff down there."

"What did they look like?" asked Rex.

"It was dark in my dream. They were small ... about the size of ten-year-old girls. They were adults though. They didn't wear tops, but they had on small cloths that were as short as miniskirts. Their hair was not straight, and it might not have been black. They saw me looking at them and looked back at me."

"Were they afraid?"

"No. They seemed not to care."

"What were they pouring?"

Thinking hard, Amber said, "I don't know. It seemed a little thicker than water ... more like light syrup or oil."

"Which of the containers were they pouring?"

Amber looked around and pointed to one in the back row.

"May I lift one?" he asked.

"Yes, but try to avoid stepping on the footprints in the dirt."

He reached above the other amphora and picked up a container. As he tipped the vessel, everyone heard the slosh of liquid! In awe, Rex replaced it carefully.

51

When the explorers returned, Britney had supper ready. Frank and the sheriff arrived and sat the table for nine. Rex settled his lanky frame at the head of the table in what Amber insisted was the guest of honor seat. Ray and Don quickly grabbed seats on either side. Everyone was smiling. If making a good impression on Rex was the goal, they scored a touchdown.

After the meal was well underway, Rex put down his fork. "Amber, may I speak freely among this group about my observations and recommendations for Trident Cave and your consortium of friends?"

She nodded.

"Frank, I am glad you are here and able to advise Amber as we go forward. The cave is of great historical value in several ways. Having been sealed from outside eyes for centuries, it is like the tombs in Egypt. Some artifacts appear to be older than those pyramids. The Pyramid Room is unique in the world. It is a pyramid within a round room with a natural light source that may have helped dictate the shape and orientation of the pyramid. Some vessels contain seeds and liquids that are hundreds or possibly thousands of years old. This area could be an archaeological wonder in itself. The pit off the Sacrificial Chamber might have a history of occupation in the layers of the pit sediment. I foresee at least ten years of active research with scientist from all over the world.

"I also see people, companies, and governments trying to wrestle it away from you by hook or crook. It will cost some money to do what I suggest. If you want to retain possession, you need to set up the foundation with a powerful board of directors immediately! You could sell it now and be rich, but if you want control and a legacy of income, advancements in science, and the pride of directing a worthwhile enterprise, a foundation is the best option."

Frank said, "Some of my colleagues saw the magazine articles and they also recommended we set up a foundation immediately."

Rex said, "Job one is setting up a foundation. Job two is absolutely securing the cave. One great value is the limited destruction of artifacts. Every time someone goes in, some history may be lost. If it is vandalized, there is no way to monetize the loss. Job three is getting a manager. Hire a manager, work them hard for a year, and pay them well. Free up your own time to get an education and see the world. You all have great ideas. Prioritize them—and put them into play. After we finish this delicious meal, I have one more recommendation."

Everyone bantered back and forth during dinner, sharing stories and quizzing Rex about his adventures and his work.

After dessert, Rex said, "When you get the foundation set up, I want to make an endowment. Doing the things we discussed will take some money. I would suggest you hold on to the personal wealth you have acquired and use the endowment fund to get started. Once monies start coming in, I can advise you more about living off the interest. I would like to make an endowment of five million dollars."

No one made a sound. Amber looked at him in disbelief.

Rex continued, "I ask that you build your own wealth and do the same for others someday. I would also be honored to serve on your board of directors and will recommend a manager—neither of which are required to receive the endowment. The endowment does not give me any control over the cave or you as the owner."

Amber looked to Frank and said, "Do you think you could work with Rex and set up a foundation? Consider naming it the Strongbox Foundation. I like the way it sounds."

Frank nodded.

Amber turned to Ray and Don and said, "What do you guys think?"

Ray said, "I like the name. Let's do it."

Don said, "If Rex will throw in a helicopter ride, I am in."

Amber walked the length of the table as Rex stood. She looked up at his eyes and hair and said, "Have you noticed we match?"

"One of the first things I noticed—and I have never been able to do anything with this mop of curls."

She gave him a big hug and motioned for Ray and Don to join in.

Everyone at the table started clapping.

The sheriff grabbed Amber's camera off the shelf and snapped a picture.

Rex gave the names of three lawyers and accountants and his recommendation for a manager. "If she works out for you, her first three months are already paid. She finished early on a project for me and is available tomorrow. I suggest you move quickly."

Amber's diary entry: "The secret to success is learning how to best make money and how to best give it away."

52

Frank moved quickly and was on the phone half the night. It was lucrative for him—and a lot of fun. Rex's manager prospect, Taylor, said she could be there in a day and stay on the job starting immediately. Taylor, answering only to her last name, sounded good on the phone and was hired on the spot.

The next day, Amber and Frank heard her coming from a mile away. When she slid her Corvette in the drive seconds later, Amber could tell that she must've been flying. Amber said, "The sheriff will probably have to speak to her soon."

Frank worked out the salary agreement. Taylor told them the first three months were covered with Rex's last job, and they had a few months to get their foundation in order. Amber offered her a bedroom, and Taylor suggested a second bedroom become an office and a place for her weights and yoga mat.

Notebook in hand, Taylor started a list and said, "I need projects, ideas, and any deadlines. What are your heart's desires?"

Amber started naming ideas and projects.

Taylor compiled list after list. "Now deadlines."

Amber said, "I want as much as possible done before school starts on August 18. Rex and Frank are sure we have trouble coming. The sooner we have things in order and the foundation functioning, the better we can survive."

"The clock is ticking. We have an hour of daylight—show me the cave entrance. We can look over the artifacts tonight."

In the morning, the farm was buzzing with activity. Taylor was directing work and making calls. A ditching machine was running power to the gate by the road to operate a remote gate opener. A ditch connected the house to the cave with water and electricity.

The next day, archaeological crews began to show up to do an accelerated excavation of the foundation of the museum that had not been finished with the university students. At least forty people were digging and screening, and ten more were documenting, tagging, and stacking labeled bags for screening.

Within a week, the foundation was poured, and the rock work begun. After the front wall was completed to the ceiling of the cave, the ironwork went in. A beautiful arched gate with a trident spear as a central motif was welded in place on massive hinges. Gates blocked all access points.

Taylor had located a potter to begin duplicating selected works from the cave. She suggested potters from all over the world would come for free to have an opportunity to be a part of history. Carole showed up to start duplicating the works. With electricity and water, she was throwing pots within hours. She set up three kilns and had assistants working to develop glazes to match the colors on the pottery. Amber supplied her with some broken pieces to assess hardness and texture. Amber gave the okay to build a primitive wood fired kiln near the cave for teaching and to get authentic effects on the pottery. Within days, more potters began to arrive.

Amber was running out of space, but Taylor arranged for a motor home to be delivered with a trailer for workspaces and offices.

Pulling Taylor aside, Amber asked, "How am I paying for all of this?"

"Rex let me use his development account until your foundation has bank accounts available, which should be any day. Frank already has his check for five million ready to deposit. You may have figured by now that I love to spend money and get maximum value for every red cent. I understand you had some challenges with robbers, kidnappers, and arsonists."

Amber replied, "Yes, it was touch-and-go, literally, for a few weeks. But each challenge made me stronger."

Taylor said, "You can have the adventure stuff. Give me a fast car and a checkbook, and I will make stuff happen. I can see trouble coming and smell a bad guy in a crowd. I've already asked one guy to leave. I paid him what we owed him and sent him packing."

"Great," Amber said. "Next time use my camera to take their picture first. The sheriff appreciates the heads-up. Look through our big album sometime. By the way, why do you go by Taylor?"

"Most people in business will do more work for a man than a woman. This sort of evens the playing field. Sometimes I don't mention the Taylor they are working for is a woman."

"I wish I were more organized like you. I love to learn and it would be amazing if I had half your skills."

Amber bent to pick up a rock to pitch out of the path and her pendant slipped out of her shirt and dangled on the leather cord. As she reached to tuck it back Taylor grabbed it from her hand. Pulling it close, Amber stumbled off balance before becoming defensive.

"Let go," she said as she pulled away, "What are you doing?"

Taylor smiled remembering the words of the monk. *"When it is time, open the mind of another like you."* Taylor reached in her own collar and pulled on a cord. She produced a glimmering gold pendant. The shape was not exactly the same but it was very similar.

"I see why you grabbed my pendant. They look alike. Ray made one for the three of us. They form a circle when put together. Where did you get yours."

Taylor pulled another necklace out into view and held it for Amber to examine. It was a gold cage with a huge brilliant ruby topped by a small slightly dented gold sphere. It was beautiful and nothing like Amber had ever seen. As she turned the Amulet over it became apparent the cage was made of the legs of bugs.

"They are scarab beetles. I had it made to look like something I once saw in another country. When I got the little gold sphere and the gold pendant, I was told to learn and someday I would become the teacher. I believe I am to teach you."

"Why don't we start working out together and you can teach me how to be organized afterwards."

"I believe I am to teach you much more than organizational skills."

*   *   *

Rex checked in frequently and sent people down to work with Taylor. He asked to come along on the next excursion into the cave to study the pyramid and Tammy's Tapestry.

When she found the hand-sized figure in the passage, it was covered in dust and dirt. Amber could not get over this strange feeling she had when looked at the cleaned-up figurine. The rust-red hair in prickly points was striking. Her stance on the small stone base was unsettling because her hands were on her hips, feet apart, just like Amber's pose a few days before she found the artifact. The torso of the figurine was not smooth like the rest of the body. The hips were covered, and the chest and back were textured. Amber was almost certain the base of the figurine was the same shape as the rock on top of the pyramid.

Amber was reluctant to open the small bottle. It was heavy, but it

did not rattle. She decided to wait until the cave excursion the next day
to open it with Rex.

Amber's diary entry: "What are your hearts desires? The one thing I
cannot have back."

53

Before the excursion, Amber gathered everyone around the picnic table. There was a flurry of activity around the mouth of the cave as the potters and builders worked.

Harry was working outside with the artifacts on the shelves and scheduled some kids to have their relics assessed. He had already identified precious stones from a dozen kids valuable enough to send them to college. Harry was every kid's new best friend. He came to the meeting at the picnic table to see what Amber had to show them.

She started by displaying the picture Tammy took of her on the pyramid: hands on hips and looking straight ahead.

Everyone agreed it was a great picture.

Amber said, "I went up there on a whim. The path up the rocks was obvious, almost familiar. Without a second thought, I dashed up there and struck a silly Wonder Woman pose. Days later, I had a dream about two women pouring something into the pit. I also had a dream about a little woman standing on top of the pyramid in only a breechcloth. Her skin looked rough and damaged. I thought my subconscious was putting me into the dream. A few days later, I was abducted and forced into the cave. I escaped and jumped the pit, which trapped the abductors. Unable to get back across the pit because of my injured ankle, I followed the passage by worming around until I found two artifacts in a painting-covered passage. One artifact was this bottle."

They passed it around, shaking, tilting, and examining it.

Don said, "It feels full."

Ray knew what was coming and nudged Rex for effect.

Amber put the figurine on the table. Nothing needed to be said.

Rex pulled a cloth from his pocket and gently picked up the artifact. He thoroughly examined it and studied the bottom.

Don said, "I don't think you'll find a 'Made in Japan' sticker on the bottom."

"No sir, I believe you are correct. And Amber, in your dream, did the little lady on the pyramid look at you?"

Amber closed her eyes and said, "Yes, but no more than the others. There were about a dozen men and women—all very small—gathered around the base of the pyramid. They were mostly women, only two or three men. When she looked at me, it seemed like she was pleased I was there."

Tammy had been snapping pictures and writing ferociously.

Amber looked over at her.

Tammy said, "This is one of those, isn't it?"

Amber nodded.

Tammy said, "Sometime, just because I know something, it doesn't mean I have to report it. Everything is not everybody's business, right, Amber?"

"Correct. Thanks, Tammy."

Amber said, "This little bottle was with the figurine. I am curious about its contents. It does not rattle, and it feels heavy."

Ray said, "Amber, do you already have an idea what's in there? It could be something bad."

"Yes, it could—but I think I was supposed to find this. I think it is important."

Don said, "We have found gems, diamonds, seeds, thick unknown goop, and sloshing liquid. Anyone want to guess what is in this one?"

Tammy said, "Maybe it is diamonds packed so tightly they cannot rattle."

Amber said, "Let's find out. In case there's a problem, I will open it away from the table. I don't expect danger. Ray, can I have your lighter? This bottle had the same wax seal as the first small bottle."

Rex handed Amber his sunglasses. "It won't hurt to shield your eyes."

Tammy was snapping pictures.

Amber stepped away and squatted. She warmed the bottleneck for a minute, dropped the lighter, and pulled on the stopper. With a squeak, it slipped from the bottle.

As everyone held their breath, a tiny puff of smoke hovered around the opening of the bottle.

Amber looked inside and went back to the picnic table.

Rex and Harry examined the stopper. The tiny dust cloud was still hovering above the bottle.

Ray said, "I think we better put the stopper back in and take it to a lab."

Rex said, "Amber, what do you think. What do you feel?"

Amber reached for the bottle and began to tip it gently to the side. She poured a small line of gray powder onto the cloth and returned the stopper to the bottle.

Harry said, "It looks like gunpowder or ashes."

Everyone agreed it looked more like ashes than anything else.

Ray looked at Amber and said, "You figured it out?"

Amber smiled, held up the tiny bottle, held the stopper in place, and tilted the bottle back and forth. There was a muffled rattle in the bottle. She said, "Anyone figure it out yet?"

They looked baffled—until they figured out the bottle was a funeral urn.

Amber said, "Ashes and teeth were all that remained after burning in the raised fireplace in front of the cave. This could be the remains of the lady at the top of the pyramid. I bet we find more if we look in the cubbyholes high on the walls of the Pyramid Room."

54

Monday came, and Amber was waiting to get on the bus. She was just another kid in a small town. In the next driveway, Ray and Don waited for the bus too. They might start waiting together, but for the first day, she wanted the bus driver to know where she lived.

Thanks to Taylor, the gates in the cave were all in place—and the house had new locks. Cave exploration was on hold for a few weeks while she started school. Taylor was full speed ahead with the museum and site excavation. Harry was busy assessing artifacts and preparing museum exhibits.

There were lots of whispers when they got on the school bus. They sat together, and Ray and Don introduced everyone to Amber. Some kids had helped in the cave and already knew her. She hoped to make lots of new friends with a goal to treat everyone in such a way as to win them over. Her related desire was to help a lot of people.

When they came back from recess, someone had drawn an excellent sketch on the chalkboard. A wild-haired girl was leaping easily over a pit as two pursuers bounced against the side of the pit. It looked like a comic book.

Amber asked who drew the sketch, but no one would tell. Amber was able to find out the name of the best artist in school. She went up to him and said, "No one will say who did the chalk drawing in homeroom, but I am told you are the best artist in school. I think the drawing is wonderful. Considering how dark it was in the cave, the blackboard is a fitting canvas. Would you mind if I take a picture of it for my album?"

He smiled and said, "You really like it?"

"Yes, I won't ever forget the leap—and your drawing captured it very well for me to share with others. Will you sign it for me?"

"Will you make me a copy of the picture and sign it for me?"

"Come sign it before it gets erased."

He rolled his wheelchair into homeroom.

Amber decided to sign the chalkboard to show her approval. The other students wanted their picture taken with Amber, the picture, and the artist.

Amber said, "If I knew someone who wanted to publish this, would you give your permission?"

His beaming smile said it all.

The teachers were not sure if Amber was going to be a distraction in class. One teacher decided to put Amber in her place the first day to show her who was in charge.

Amber smiled and complied with every request.

The teacher chose an exceptionally difficult question and really put Amber on the spot.

Amber knew the answer, but she also knew answering it would make the teacher try to make it more difficult for her. Amber wrote the correct answer on a piece of paper, signed it, and said, "You have chosen a tough one. May I research it and report tomorrow?"

The teacher, feeling the upper hand and having put Amber in her place, agreed and dismissed class. As Amber walked near, the teacher smiled and said, "I will expect an answer tomorrow."

Amber smiled, handed her the paper, and said, "Is now okay?" She walked out with a polite wave.

The teacher realized Amber had allowed her to save face by appearing to be confounded by the question. She decided to give the girl a chance. Little Miss Amber might be okay.

School was easy for the Trio. They were smart and studied together at times. As a result, they were often the top three students in their classes. The Trio did not compete in class. School was fun, but they could hardly wait to get back to their other activities. Though they were all athletic, they decided to only do track. Amber's chalkboard sketch ended up in the school annual and in a local magazine. Her new friend, Wally, even got some royalties for the artwork. Amber asked him to draw a map of the cave for the museum and the fliers.

After school, it was adventure time. During the day, they planned their next adventure. When Britney had time, she liked to help set up the museum. She had a talent for organization. People were coming from all over to see the artifacts. A sampling of items were taken from the cave and displayed in the museum. Large pictures of the gold nugget on the stalagmite and the bowl in the stalagmite were prominent. The bear skeleton was assembled and towered in a corner. They held a contest to see who could come up with the best explanation for the artifacts in the cracked dirt pit. There were some outrageous ideas.

A crew of archeologists planned to set up a dig in the cracked dirt pit during the winter. The artifacts from there might help answer some questions. With the cave and museum settled down, Amber, Ray, and Don were ready for new adventures.

55

In a bail hearing, Victor Deal withdrew his confession on the grounds that he was hypothermic and not represented by an attorney. He was released on bail and scheduled to appear for trial. He knew if he was ever on trial, he would go to jail for a long time.

A warrant was out for the arrest of George Gomez for arson and attempted murder but most everyone thought he was in Mexico. Both men wanted to settle a score with Amber Preston. When George heard Victor was out on bail, he contacted him about going after the treasure. Knowing they would have to leave the country, they planned an escape to Mexico. George had the connections, and Victor had the money.

The plan was to steal all the artifacts they could get from the house and museum, and set explosives to destroy Amber and the cave. Victor would make sure they had vehicles staged along the way to get across the border. George had access to dynamite and timers. Knowing the Crum brothers would want revenge; Victor stopped by the hospital and hinted at what they planned. Both men were in body casts and listened to Victor's ravings.

*   *   *

Two days later, at midnight, two men dressed in black parked quietly by the gate and walked to the house.

Amber was alone since Taylor went to her apartment for most weekends. When Amber heard someone breaking in the back door, she escaped through the front—and into the iron grasp of George Gomez. He tied her hands and led her back inside.

Victor started loading bags with artifacts from the china cabinet. In the bedroom, he flipped the mattress and found her hidden money.

George gagged her and found the wall switch to open the gate. After grabbing the keys from the wall, he led her toward the cave.

Victor brought in the car, and they unloaded the packs and lights and found the key to the museum.

Amber hoped they would take some of the artifacts and be gone.

They filled bags with treasures and put them in the trunk.

Amber thought they might put her in the trunk or throw her, tied up, into the river, but they had more dramatic plans.

After forcing her to climb the ladder to the upper level, they marched her to the back of the cave.

Amber was not too concerned. *How much can two people carry?*

They stopped in the Pyramid Room, and Victor left a pack there. In the Sacrificial Chamber, George removed a device with a timer from his pack. While he was working with it, Victor tied Amber's hands behind her back. He reached into her pocket and removed her knife. He put a few smaller artifacts in the bag, and George said he was ready.

Amber saw a timer counting down on the metal box. It was set for fifteen minutes.

George set the box among the ceramic containers on the side of the path.

The magnitude of their plan was sinking in for Amber. They were going to blow up the cave, its artifacts, and her. A hundred plans had gone through her head during the past twenty minutes—but none of them included bombs.

In the Pyramid Room, they set the timer on another bomb for fourteen minutes. They tied her feet and left her on the ground. They set the bomb at the edge of the path, and like before, George gave her a good kick in the side before leaving her in the dark. They hurried out of the room.

Amber screamed threats at them as their lights faded. Soon it was completely dark except for the little clock counting down on the box next to her.

56

At the sheriff's office, a caller insisted someone was trying to kill Amber Preston.

The deputy on duty drove by and found the back door open and a pry bar by the door. He called for backup.

The blue lights on a dark night reflected in the windows of the Spark house, and Don woke up in time to see them. Seeing the police car across the fields, he got dressed and shouted for his parents. He was out the door and headed across the field before anyone else was dressed.

A car with its lights off sped away from the cave and toward the police cruiser as Don stepped onto Amber's porch. He reached inside and flipped the switch to close the gate.

The deputy ran over and pointed his gun at Don.

With his hands in the air, Don said, "I am the neighbor. The bad guys are driving away, but I shut the gate."

There was a screech of metal as the car wedged in the gate as it was closing.

Sirens screamed on the highway. The deputy sent gravel flying as he spun toward the gate. Sliding in front of the trapped car, a second squad car blocked any hope of escape. Once the two men were cuffed, the officers checked the car and the trunk for Amber. About the time they concluded Amber was not in the car or the trunk, there was a terrible explosion. Fire and smoke belched out of the cave, and the ground shook.

Everyone rushed to the cave, except the officer who was locking the prisoners in the back seat of his cruiser. Don turned on lights around the cave. Debris, dirt, and rocks were scattered around the mouth of the cave. Ray and Ben went to the remnant of the destroyed ladder to the upper level, but the passage was blocked with fallen rock.

Ray and Don went to get their cave gear and prepared to look for Amber. They took extra gear for her, ropes, and medical supplies. The best chance of entry was from the river gate or through the core-drilled opening into the crypt.

Ray found the bundle of cave keys on the museum floor. The river passage was most direct, and they hurried down the path to the gate. Ben followed, planning to stay at the gate to relay messages and watch for their return. An ambulance was called in case Amber was injured.

Don and Ray could not get to the gate because rock and dirt were all around it. The explosion had caused a cave-in and landslide that blocked the gate.

They returned to the mouth of the cave and went to the bored hole in the crypt. Leaving the keys with Ben, they hurried through the opening. They crawled through the tight passage with their extra gear. They checked the passage that ended at the river gate, but there was no sign of Amber. The passage was full of rock and breakdown. In the bottom of the sacrificial pit, they caught their breath and climbed the fifty-foot ladder.

Almost everything was in order at the top. A few stalactites had fallen, but there was very little destruction. They called for Amber but heard no reply. When they came to Tammy's Tapestry, they saw breakdown ahead. The tapestry was as far as they could go. The mural was still intact and undamaged, but the ceiling had fallen beyond it and blocked the path completely.

After shouting for Amber for a few minutes, they returned to the mouth of the cave through the crypt.

The sheriff was there, and they gave him a report. The upper level of the cave was blocked near Tammy's Tapestry. Don marked it on a map for the sheriff. Ray suggested getting his friend to bring his backhoe and dig out the side passage.

The sheriff asked if it looked like a cave-in. Don explained about the explosions and the fire and smoke coming out of the cave. The car had been pulled from the gate, and the stolen artifacts were logged and checked in as evidence. Frank had been called, and he worked with the sheriff to make sure the evidence was secure and not damaged.

Tammy showed up and started writing the story.

Ray had an idea. After loading up with candy bars and water, he and Don went up to the bluff. It was difficult to find in the dark, but they finally located the area where the daytime light entered the Pyramid Room. Ray shouted into the opening, and Don tied a spare flashlight to a rope. He lowered it down until it touched a rock and raised it back up a few feet. He tied it to a root and dropped two candy bars through the hole.

Back at the cave, they discussed their options. No one knew if she was even in the cave. No one wanted to believe she could be in the river.

The backhoe showed up before daylight, and the rescue squad was there on standby. The backhoe started carefully moving rock out to the front of the cave. Reaching beyond the recently collapsed area, he started clearing debris out of the side passage. When there was a little space above the breakdown, Ray and Don climbed the rock pile to see if they could get through. They moved over the top, zigzagged around boulders, and climbed down the back of the breakdown.

Instead of coming out in the upper passage, they were in a new room. It was a broad room with a flat floor like the main cave. Don told Ray to turn off his lights. Bits of light twinkled through the wall to the right. A close examination revealed stacked rock. They were seeing light through the cracks in the stacked wall. The light was from the cars outside. Don moved a rock and created a head-sized opening in the bluff, looking right out at the cars and people. He shouted to the sheriff who was in the small crowd outside. Ray told the sheriff through the little opening that they were going to see if there was a route through the upper level. They asked him to have a truck back up to the bluff and be prepared to help them exit when they returned.

The room looked like ancient living space, and multiple passages led back into the bluff. They called for Amber, but there was no answer. They decided the most likely place to find Amber was in the upper level.

They crawled back up the breakdown and moved toward the back of the pile of rubble. After moving many rocks, they made headway and were moving down another side of the rubble. This time, it looked familiar. They were not far from where the ladder had passed through the floor. Huge boulders covered the entire area. They jogged toward the Pyramid Room and called Amber's name.

Ray saw his flashlight dangling from a rope over the pyramid, and Don saw Amber. She was barely inside the Pyramid Room, facedown, with bits of rock and dirt on her. She was breathing. They gently shook her and called her name. She moved. As they continued to try to rouse her, she became more active. It was soon apparent that she could not hear. She sat up, drank lots of water, and ate some candy. Her eyes did not look right, but nothing seemed to be broken.

One on each side, they carried her to the front of the cave and helped her crawl over the breakdown. She had not said a word. The sheriff had moved more rocks and had a big truck backed up to the bluff so they could walk onto the flatbed.

Everyone cheered as the Trio emerged from the side of the bluff.

Amber went to the hospital. They respected her privacy and kept her covered so her scars did not show. Within a few days, her voice and hearing improved. Though she had a concussion, no permanent damage was expected. There was a huge bundle of flowers from Taylor and Rex. The boys were arguing about who got to push her in the wheelchair to the car.

When they got back to the house, Taylor was busy getting everything back to normal. Get-well cards were stacked on the table. A simple one on hospital stationery said, "Wish I had called a bit sooner. We decided to take you up on your offer. See you after rehab." Now she knew who called and alerted the sheriff she was in danger. Amber smiled and had that great feeling inside that she had grown to love.

* * *

Everyone gathered around the table at the Sharp house for dinner. Tammy wanted to know what happened in the cave. Amber recounted the entire adventure to the point she was tied and left on the floor with two bombs set to go off.

Ray said, "If the bombs were set in the Pyramid Room and the Sacrificial Chamber, why was there no damage to those rooms?"

Don said, "You got free and moved the bombs, didn't you?"

"I managed to get to Ray's stash of supplies and used a knife to cut free. Taking the flashlight, I carried one bomb and the rope to the Sacrificial Chamber and got the other bomb. I tied them together and hung the rope across my shoulder while I climbed the ladder to the pit and ran to the river. I threw both bombs through the bars and into the water. With only minutes remaining, I got as far away as possible. It turns out that was a mistake. A third bomb must have been set near the front of the cave. When I passed the Pyramid Room, the passage lit up ahead of me. I only woke up when you found me."

Britney said, "Well, you certainly saved the cave and yourself. If the bombs had gone off where they were planned, little would remain to be studied."

Amber said, "Can we eat now? I'm starved."

Ray said, "Amber is back."

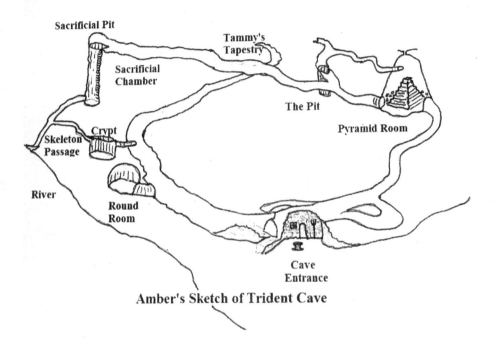

Amber's Sketch of Trident Cave

EPILOGUE

Ray and Don got up early one fall Saturday and did their chores around the house and farm. They checked in with their mom and headed over to see Amber. When they went to her house, she was not there. They walked back by the barn and down to the cave and found her sitting on a picnic table by the river.

They sat across from her and asked what she was doing.

Amber said, "I have never been fishing and was thinking about a fishing trip.

Don said, "There are plenty of fish to catch right off the bank at your own place. Why would you take a trip?"

"I was thinking about another fishing trip I read about in literature class." She summarized *The Old Man and the Sea* for Ray and Don since they had never read it. "An old fisherman loved to fish and met his adversary, a large fish that nearly got the best of him. In the end he got home with only a skeleton. We put a lot of ourselves into this cave and had a lot of fun too. I hope we don't ever get so obsessed with this that we forget to have fun and help others."

The boys agreed, and Don said, "Let's get some food and go fishing. Ray is not much of a fisherman, but I will be glad to show you how it's done."

Ray rolled his eyes and said, "Let's fish till noon, and whoever catches the most doesn't have to clean them."

Amber said, "I will cook. We can have a fish fry tonight."

"What if you invite people and don't catch any fish?" asked Ray.

"Then we compromise. We fish until ten thirty, and if we have enough by then, I will call everyone while you two fish till noon to see who is the best fisherman."

Thirty minutes later, they were back with fishing poles and bait. They set up some lawn chairs near the edge of the water. Amber was on the left side because she was left handed, and they wanted to avoid getting a fishhook in the ear.

While Don got some rod and reels ready, Ray showed Amber the basics of casting a closed-face reel.

All baited up, Ray and Don cast the lines into the river. The river was slow and deep near the bank. Their lines sank at an angle far across the river.

Remembering what Ray said about casting, Amber cast hard over her head. Both boys ducked as the hook and bait sailed high overhead near the tree limbs and plopped in the water a few feet in front of her chair.

They all laughed. Amber began reeling in the extra line. By the time she got the slack reeled in, she had a bite—and the line was being pulled out into the river.

Don said, "Set the hook."

Ray said, "Reel it in."

Amber was excited and held on as the pole bent over.

Ray's pole made a noise, and the tip bent toward the water. Don jumped up to help Amber by setting the drag. He handed it back to her and said, "Now reel it in."

Amber reeled. When the fish turned back across the river, her reel would click and screech.

Don was getting a bite, and Ray was reeling in his big bluegill and getting it on a stringer.

Amber was fighting with her fish. It would come in, and she would reel. It would swim and pull line back out.

Ray waited to help Amber land her fish before putting his line back out. As the fish neared the bank, Ray grabbed the line and pulled it close to the edge where he stood. As he lifted it near the surface, he could see why it had taken her so long to land. This twelve-pound channel catfish could easily break the line or bite it in two. Being careful of the spines, he grabbed the fish by the gill opening and dragged it out of the water.

Don was landing a smaller catfish at the same time. They all congratulated each other on their catches and put them on the stringer. Amber agreed it was beginner's luck, and they all had their lines back in the water in minutes. They caught catfish, bass, bluegill, and even a gar. By ten thirty, they had plenty to confirm a fish fry.

Amber went to make some calls, and Ray and Don continued the competition. Britney brought over a big pot to fit on the gas grill and a few gallons of oil. She had a recipe for a good fish batter and hush puppies. They called friends and set dinner for six o'clock with horseshoes and rook.

Even though Don technically had more keepers than Ray, there were so many fish they both stayed busy cleaning and cutting them up. It was the best fishing day either of them could remember. After they filleted the big catfish, they were reminded of Amber's story. They saved the skeleton to clean up and have one more memory to go on Amber's shelf.

The crowd started arriving at five thirty, and the fish was already coming off the grill. The sheriff said he wasn't invited, but he followed all the speeding traffic. Tammy and her new photographer were there.

Ms. Smith from Child Protective Services came and brought pies. Three of their teachers, Wally and his dad, a van full of classmates, and several other people in the community showed up too. Harry even drove up from Huntsville. One of the rescue squad guys showed up and the core-drilling man came a little late. Tammy took lots of pictures and even took one of Amber holding up the catfish skeleton. Everyone had so much fun talking and telling stories. The sheriff beat everyone at horseshoes until Taylor stepped up to the pit. The rook game ended with the older players winning everything.

When the impromptu party was winding down, Britney said, "This is what the community needs: a good social and fish fry."

Amber had a look in her eye. "Well, I guess we should make it happen occasionally. We could put a few benches and some picnic tables down by the cave. In case we can't always catch fish, we could put some in the freezer. Maybe we could put a horseshoe pit or two down in the flat area and have a little shelter."

The crunch of gravel in the driveway interrupted her planning and signaled a new arrival. A shiny Cadillac pulled up, and Preston, Sheila, and Lisa got out of the car. Everyone cheered as Amber sprinted to hug them. Lisa looked much better. She had gained some weight and her hair was beginning to grow back. It was the same color as Amber's unruly auburn curls.

"What in the world is going on here?" asked Preston.

Amber said, "I learned how to fish today, and we are having a little fish fry for a few close friends. You are just in time."

Lisa and Amber sat on the porch and talked while Preston and Sheila mingled with the crowd.

The summer had been so exciting. As Ray and Don headed her way, Amber wondered what other adventures were just around the corner. She did not have to wait long to find out.

Frank drove up minutes later and joined the festivities, but he asked for a meeting after the party.

Amber, Preston, the Sparks, Taylor, and Frank met for about an hour. Some big problems loomed ahead. There had been an attempt by the federal government to condemn the property take it over under the pretense of a threat of disease. The Strongbox Foundation was in place and the lawyers had stopped the initial takeover attempt. Frank had a plan to try to put up some more legal roadblocks. Amber signed off on a pile of papers, and Frank went to Nashville to meet with Rex's lawyers.

Amber, Ray, and Don went to the picnic table by the cool river and looked up at the stars.

Amber lifted her brass pendant necklace and held it up to the starlight. She said, "Ray, when you made these for us as a team, I bet you had no idea the excitement we would see."

Don said, "I've never had so much fun in my life, but it gets scary at times."

Ray said, "Amber, do you regret anything?"

"Just that I was mad at my mom before I knew she had cancer—and maybe that I planted those tree seeds so close to the house. Either of you guys have any ideas what adventures to plan next?"

Don said, "Adventure will probably find us."

AFTERWORD

This is book two of a four book, Yellow Fever, series. Book one, Yellow Fever, The Caged Ruby, introduces us to Taylor and Rex and their adventures that span the globe. Their philanthropic quests take them from mystical monasteries to archeological digs and Egyptian tombs. At every turn they must deal with those who want to do them harm and get their treasure.

WWW.Rodneysylerbooks.com

*   *   *

I have an idea to do a crowd sourced book in the future. If you want to be a part of a new kind of novel where you contribute an idea or an event, look on WWW.Rodneysylerbooks.com for a place to sign up to participate.

An Excerpt from the Next Book in the Series

As Amber got settled in school and was ready to leave the phenomenal discoveries in the cave to the experts for a few weeks, it all hit the fan. The potential value of the discovery, in the minds of four different entities, was in the billions. Some even considered it to be a matter of national security. In no case did they intend to leave the decisions in the hands of a fourteen-year-old kid. By hook or crook, they each had plans to take over Trident Cave, and the treasure within.

KEEP READING FOR AN EXCITING EXCERPT FROM
THE NEXT NOVEL IN THE YELLOW FEVER SERIES,

YELLOW FEVER,
AMBER'S INTUITION

CHAPTER 1

Amber's home Middle Tennessee fall 1975

Drenched in sweat in a tangle of sheets, Amber woke from the recurring nightmare. She was in the Pyramid Room in the cave. It wasn't really her, but a little wild haired cave woman who looked like her. The nightmare always ended this way. A saber tooth tiger terrorized the village for weeks picking off her friends in the woods or the river. Days would go by and he would return without warning. Now he found his way into the caverns and the pyramid room. Even when they put up barricades at the entrance, he just ripped them down. Their only escape was to climb to the high tiny passages that were too small for him to enter.

Each dream ended the same. As the tiger tore through the cave, people scattered. If they were fast enough, they climbed to safety. Sometimes Amber would wake from her dream while being chased around the pyramid.

Amber drank some water and saw the light on in the hallway. She went out to find Taylor still awake in the office reading. As Amber watched from the door unseen, Taylor flipped the pages of the encyclopedia slowly as if looking at pictures. Many pages had no pictures. *"Could she be reading that fast?"*

Taylor looked up from the volume. "What are you doing up? You're all wet. What is going on?"

"I keep having dreams."

"About the cave?"

"Yes. It's basically the same dream over and over. Each time there is more detail and it gets scarier. I feel like I am supposed to do something."

"By the way, when you were looking at the encyclopedia just now, were you reading?"

Taylor said, "Well not in a conventional sense. I was more skimming and looking at the pictures."

"How could you get anything out of it going so fast?"

"The truth is, I don't let many people know this about me because they tend to constantly test me. But since you are my student, I will share a secret. I have what is called eidetic memory. It is what some call photographic memory. Now if you are like most people, you will ask me to prove it."

"No. I suspected you had some special gifts. Managing the operations you made elaborate lists of things to do. Then you rarely looked back at them, and yet you got everything done. I had a feeling that you were special from the day we hired you."

"Once I saw your pendant, I was sure it was my job to teach you as much as I could."

They both subconsciously reached for the pendants. Amber's pendant was brass and made from a rare and valuable twenty dollar coin. The coin had been sawed into three identical oddly curved pendants for Amber, Don, and Ray. To Amber, it was priceless.

Taylor's pendant had quite a different providence. She received it as a gift from a Monk when she had completed a challenge and brought back a tiny gold sphere. Seeing a similar pendant on Amber, she knew the Monk's prediction had come to pass. He had said, "Now you are the student, keep your mind open always. When it is time, open the mind of another like you."

Feeling sleepy again, Amber went back to bed. She lay there a while thinking about how to catch a tiger. After drifting off to sleep, the dream came back. This time Amber was carrying broad leaves past the pyramid room to a deep pit. She and two other ladies pulled a long makeshift ladder from the pit. The leaves were placed over thin sticks to form a cover over it. One small pole was angled across the hole on top of the leaves. The red haired lady tested the small pole by putting one foot on it. It held her weight easily. She stepped back and carrying the small torch, led the other ladies away and back to the pyramid.

They ate and jabbered some odd language until screams came from near the cave entrance. Everyone scattered up the sides of the rock walls and into small cave openings except Amber. As the last man came running into the pyramid room Amber moved closer to the exit that led to the pit. The cave was dark except for a faint light from above and one or two torches. The tiger did not need light to track the humans who had scurried up the sides. He leaped high up one of the rock faces trying to grab a woman peeking out of a cave. When he regained footing, he looked around the room and spotted Amber.

Without even a pause he sprung for her. A thousand pounds of rage and fury launched in her direction. Like a streak she disappeared around the corner with the little torch in hand. She only had seconds ahead of his claws and teeth when she came to the pit. With her lead foot she hit the small pole at full speed. The spring vaulted her over the pit. She did not miss a step on the other side and ran straight for the tiny passage that would shield her from his long paws if he cleared the pit. Roaring snarls of pain and rage erupted from the pit. A terrible thrashing came from below but she remained safe in her tunnel.

She knew he could bound side to side and probably claw his way out if he was not badly injured. After a while when it was totally quiet she slid out and eased over to the edge of the pit. Carefully sneaking a look over the edge, a terrifying scream came from below and a flurry of movement. Amber's own screams woke her. Taylor was at her door in seconds.

"Nightmare again?"

"Yes, but maybe the last one. In the dream, before I woke myself screaming, a huge saber-toothed tiger was impaled with a bloody black spear point protruding from his back."

"And I suppose you had something to do with the tiger's capture in the dream?"

"I was the bait for the trap."

"Let's hope that was only a dream and not a premonition of things to come."

CHAPTER 2

Middle Tennessee spring 1976

A mber was 15 years old and the owner of a nice quiet farm in Middle Tennessee. Well it was nice and quiet today, but if the past was any predictor of the future, it would not stay quiet very long.

Over the last year Amber lost her brother to a fire, nearly lost her mother to cancer, and she was on a first name basis with the local rescue squad. But on the other hand, she had inherited a large farm, found gold, artifacts, and jewels in the cave, made great friends, and had become one of the most well-known and wealthiest people in town.

The cave turned out to be an archaeological wonder that drew worldwide attention of scientists, researchers, as well as all sorts of very bad people. Now big companies and even the government wanted to take it all away from her. At fifteen, when she should be thinking about boys and dating, she was fighting for her livelihood and her life.

Amber was not alone. She had her two great friends Don and Ray Spark who lived on the farm just across the field. Her official guardians were Ben and Linda Spark and her grandfather who went by his last name Preston.

Amber hired an incredible Corvette driving hottie as a business manager who was supremely organized and loved to spend money. Taylor managed the construction of a museum in the mouth of the cave, an archeological dig, and oversaw the construction of a small Research Institute along the hillside adjacent to the cave. Of Taylor's boyfriends around the world, the Aussie Arborist Mick captured her heart.

The farm, cave, and treasures were set up in a foundation called The Strongbox Foundation. Amber just wanted to share the wealth, help others, and preserve the cave as an ongoing source of revenue. Since they found some ancient seeds in containers and some toxic smelling goo in some of the jars, the federal government wanted to take control and evaluate the seeds for possible crop advancements and control any potential viruses or bacteria that might be present in the containers. So naturally they had the FBI snooping around trying to develop a reason to go in and take whatever samples they needed and lock it down.

At the same time, a foreign seed and agricultural conglomerate had spies infiltrating the operation for some of the same financial reasons. They knew if they could get their hands on seeds thousands of years old, they might make genetic changes and dominate markets. If they could patent the changes, then all the better.

And then there were the really bad guys.

Amber talked to her lawyer Frank and suggested they offer to let one FBI agent into their operation to see what they were doing. She reasoned, rather than risk an all-out raid where all their stuff would be damaged or destroyed, they should invite one or two agents to work alongside them.

Frank relented and brought in the FBI Special Agent in Charge (SAC). They negotiated a plan where an agent and a pathogen specialist from USAMRID would spends a few days with Amber in the cave. They signed documents declaring that any discoveries made were the property of The Strongbox Foundation. Ray, Don, and Amber were excited to get to work with real FBI agents.

The next day a black car pulled up to the house and a well-dressed man and woman emerged and stood looking around through dark glasses. Amber asked them to come to the porch and sit for a while. She brought out ice tea and a stack of papers. They each showed an ID and presented her with a business card.

Taylor came to the porch and introduced herself as Amber's business manager. She passed a form to each of them to sign as she checked their signatures against their badges. The USAMRID lady commented that she was surprised the lawyer was not present to handle the documents. Amber said, "He is just inside, I told him we would call him in if we needed him. You see, I don't distrust you. I think you will do what is right. If there are pathogens, I would rather our government have them than an enemy government. If there are seeds that would benefit our country, I would want them to do just that, and extend whatever value to other countries in need. I don't want someone to take something and make things that will do harm. Now I know you have a job to do so I hope you brought some more clothes. Drive down to the cave and you can change there."

Amber introduced them to Ray, Don, and Tammy the reporter and photographer. With a map of the cave Amber pointed out all the known passages and described their contents. She said, "Since the bombing there is a cave-in that divides the upper level. We can enter the Sacrificial Chamber from the lower level and the Pyramid Room from the newly discovered front rooms. Where do you want to go first? This will be a working trip for us but we can work in either room.

Special Agent Fife said, "Let's start in the pyramid room. I have been fascinated by that since I read your article."

Don said, "Dr. Winter, should we call you Doctor or Colonel?"

"Colonel Winter is fine."

Ray said, "I am glad you brought your medical bag, Amber and Don tend to get scraped up sometime."

Don said, "Who fell in the pit and had to get pulled out?"

Amber said, "I bet you have test equipment in the bag don't you?"

"Mostly, however I do try to be prepared for small accidents. I have some bandages, antiseptic, and suturing equipment."

Tammy said, "Maybe we won't need it. Is everyone ready to go, I am ready for a new adventure."

Special Agent Fife said, "I would appreciate it if you did not take my picture while we are here. I try to keep a low profile in case I have to go undercover."

"If I get you in some pictures I will make sure I crop you out when I process the pictures. Why don't you take the group picture then and let's get going."

They maneuvered over the breakdown and were soon moving along the upper level passage. Amber showed them the mirrors used for guiding passage without lights. When they entered the pyramid room, Colonel Winter asked, "Is this where you were injured by the blast when the robbers attempted to destroy the cave."

"Yes, that was quite a night. We almost lost it all."

Special Agent Fife said, "From what I read, you picked up bombs and ran them to the river to save the cave, but did not know about the third bomb. We had explosives training, but I know a lot of trained men and women who would have gotten as far away from the bombs as possible."

"A year ago, I would have run away. After getting burned and going through physical therapy and the burn treatment, I changed. I decided to live and make a difference. I worked hard and changed myself physically too. Enough about me, let's look for some treasure."

Amber told them the story of finding the little figurine and the tiny bottle in the high passage on the other side of the pyramid. They looked around at nearly a hundred small cubby holes carved into the rock walls around the pyramid. She said, "I think some of the other cubby holes will have bottles in them and maybe some new passages."

Tammy said, "You could go back to the top of the pyramid and look around for things in the cubby holes. Take the big light where you can see across the room."

Without discussion she sprinted to the top without missing a step. Standing on the top, she again felt like the Wonder Woman super hero. She shone the light around the room and soon spotted some candidates. With the light beam she directed Ray to climb to the first one.

"This one is full of bottles. I can't easily climb down with them though. How about I put some in my pack and lower them to Don?"

Tammy said, "Take pictures first. Amber, take one from there too."

Soon tiny bottles were lowered to the path and Colonel Winter was suiting up. She prepared bags to seal the bottles and labelled them. Amber spotted a few more bottles in the other little cave entrances and came down.

"Before you bag those, may I see them?"

Amber examined each bottle. Most were small like the one she had found in the passage. One was slightly larger but unusually long. She shook each one and spent extra time on the long bottle. It finally occurred to Amber what made the bottle interesting. The top was almost as large as the diameter.

Amber said, "This is something different." She shook it gently and could feel a slight shift inside but nothing rattled around. The bottle was unusually heavy.

Colonel Winter said, "Any idea what is inside based on what you have seen before?"

"No. This is something special. It is probably packed with broken shells like some others we have found. A scientist told us that they crushed the shells, heated them to drive out all the moisture and when cool used them to absorb moisture in the container. It works like those little packets of silica gel that come in shoe boxes."

Amber updated some sketches and said, "If you take this container, can you x-ray it to see what is inside?"

Colonel Winter said, "It won't be real clear going through ceramic but we will try. May we take these other containers also?"

"Sure, but treat them with respect. They very likely contain the ashes and teeth of the people who built this pyramid and lived here. You might learn something from the teeth. In these small bottles the seal can usually be loosened with some heat."

Special Agent Fife said, "How valuable are these?"

"Documented artifacts from this cave are going in museums all around the world. Without even knowing what is in the long flask, we could get thousands of dollars a year as a loan to a museum. I have a feeling the long bottle will be in its own exhibit. We may keep that one here in the museum."

"What if it is full of ashes?"

"It won't be. I don't know exactly what is in there, but it is special. I just have a feeling."

Ray said, "My money is on Amber. Her intuition is pretty good."

Don said, "I suppose you are going to open it in a controlled environment to make sure there are no diseases like Yellow Fever." He winked at Amber as he used their code word for Gold Fever.

Agent Fife said, "We know about your code word for Gold Fever. We are the FBI. We have researched you well and talked to a lot of your friends and a few enemies."

"Good, then just let us know if you want to know something new. I bet Colonel Winter still wants to know more."

"Yes. If you tell too much, I will let you know. This is extremely interesting and informative. Unlike the FBI, I am rather uninformed. I want to focus on any possibility there may be contagions among the artifacts. The reports of your and Ray's recent illness was unsettling."

"I suppose Agent Fife forgot to share with you that we figured out where we got exposed."

Colonel Winter turned to Agent Fife, "This is probably not the best place for a discussion but when we are alone, you have some explaining to do. I deal in facts, if you are holding out on me or wasting my time, you can plan on a new much less comfortable assignment."

"They think they got the bug from a girl they met in Colorado. It has not been verified."

"We were with her a week before we got sick. She got sick a few days before us with the same symptoms. Like with us, it passed in a few days."

Ray said, "Some people think the government is trying to fabricate a disease risk so they can confiscate the cave and the treasures. Agent Fife, what do you think about that theory?"

"It is absurd. We only want the truth."

"Then come over here. See these stains on the rock at the base of the pyramid? Have a seat next to it and I will tell you a story."

"I will stand for the story."

Bending to pick up a smaller dark stained rock Ray attempted to hand it to Agent Fife but he backed away.

Amber said, "Well maybe he does think there is something dangerous here. Maybe his bosses have not told him everything."

Don said, "I think we know where everyone stands now." He picked up a medium size jar like the one broken when Amber was kidnapped. He tossed it near the Agent and it broke into pieces. Black syrup-like material spilled across the rocks. Yellow foam bubbled up wherever it touched the stones. Both agents backed away. The foaming increased in speed and soon all the black material was bubbling yellow.

"This was my inspiration for 'Yellow Fever'. It was either that or the Black Plague or the Spanish Flu. I was making it up as I went to scare the Crums."

She dipped her finger into the bubbles and held it up. "We had this tested. It is concentrated sodium hydroxide mostly." She wiped it off with some dirt and went on with her speech. "Colonel Winter, please take a sample back to test."

After the samples were collected, Amber suggested they exit and enter the Sacrificial Chamber through The Cript. While in the Cript, a room Amber discovered months earlier with Civil War soldiers and Gold treasure, Special Agent Fife asked questions about the bodies of the soldiers and if the skeletons had been located. Amber sensed he was testing another possible reason for Federal involvement.

"I am sure you have read the sheriff's report. Nothing has changed since then."

As instructed by Amber, Tammy took pictures of everything, especially the agents looking around in each room. Amber's attorney Frank wanted documentation of the expedition in case there was any question later.

They climbed the ladder to the top of the sacrificial pit and as all first time visitors, both agents were awestruck by the room. Aside from the natural beauty of the stalactites and cave features, the array of pottery and rows of tiny footprints were amazing. After Amber gave them a few minutes to absorb the scene, she suggested they go to Tammy's Tapestry where the passage ended in breakdown from the explosions. "Tammy, will you lead the way?"

Down the steps and through a corridor Tammy brought the group to a halt. Turning to the group she said, look behind you. All lights turned and darted coming to rest on what Amber had named, Tammy's Tapestry. A beautiful mural of colors and hundreds of figures spanned high above the tunnel they had just come through.

"Feel free to take pictures. We have experts all over the world trying to make sense of all this. The leading theory is that different groups occupied this space over time. They wrote their story over the history that was recorded earlier. Bits and pieces still remain of the earliest work but much is lost."

There was a crack and rumble behind them. Dirt and rock fell from the ceiling above the breakdown.

Don said, "That is our cue to leave. This ceiling is not stable since Victor tried to kill Amber by blowing up the cave."

Before Colonel Winter could move forward closer to the group, a boulder slid from the pile of rubble behind her. Amber sprinted and took the unsuspecting lady off her feet and six feet to the side as they piled into the dirt. The boulder lay right where Colonel Winter had been standing. More rubble rolled down the mound as Amber helped the Colonel to her feet. "Sorry I tackled you. Are you ok? We need to get further away from this area."

"No need for an apology. That rock would have crushed my legs. I was staring over at the Tapestry and didn't see the boulder coming. Thank you."

As Don and Ray passed the slab of rock to help Amber and the Colonel back to safety, Ray stopped. "Tammy, come get a picture of this."

The top surface of the rock was covered in colorful designs and figures. Along the edges, figures were incomplete where the rock had broken from a larger slab. Everyone shined their flashlights to the ceiling where the rock seemed to have originated. No drawings adorned the ceiling. A gaping hole opened into a vast room. Amber used a large flashlight and shined it through the new opening. High overhead the vaulted ceiling was covered in colorful drawings.

As they hurried out of the breakdown area, Amber said, "It feels good to be part of a new discovery? Colonel, I usually name features and passages the first thing that comes to mind at the time of the discovery. I think if we can get it stable, we can ascend the pile of rocks and gain access to that room and likely a third level of the cave. Let's call it the 'Winter's Ascension'. It sounds better than 'The Place Where a Boulder Almost Broke Colonel Winter's Leg.'"

Don said, "Can we name the pit 'The Pit Where Ray Fell In a Hole?'"

Ray said, "That is not funny, I could have died."

Amber said, "I am thinking of calling it 'Ray's Faux Pas,' it's French for Ray's step in the wrong direction."

When they reached the Sacrificial Chamber, Amber suggested Colonel Winter select an item that might contain a dangerous pathogen.

"There is no way of knowing without examination in a lab."

Don said, "Then what can you do to convince the government to leave us alone and quit trying to take the cave from Amber. I know you work for the government and have to obey orders but what you are doing is wrong. It would be better if you helped us protect what we have from others that are trying to steal it.

"What others?" Again she looked at Special Agent Fife.

He said, "There are two groups we have identified who have financial interest in the cave. One is an Asian Agricultural Conglomerate. They specialize in monopolizing certain seed stocks and forcing customers to pay extra because the genetics are patented. They are known to go to any lengths to get what they want. Early on, they made a substantial offer to buy the entire property."

Amber said, "I turned it down."

Ray had been unusually quiet on this trip in the cave. He said. "I agree with Don. I thought you were like policemen who were here to protect and serve. I looked up your motto, Fidelity, Bravery, Integrity. Can you be those things and sneak around and try to take away the cave?"

Colonel Winter addressed the question. "USAMRID's motto is a bit different. 'Biodefense Solutions to Protect Our Nation.' My job is to help keep our nation safe. From what Amber said earlier, that is her wish also. What we are finding here today makes me feel a lot better about the biological safety of the artifacts in the cave. Are there those who would like to make a big media splash about the risk here and take over the operation? Absolutely. I happen to know some very influential people who can, and will, keep those people in line. In fact, I predict full cooperation in the near future. Amber, I do have one favor to ask. I may need you to come meet my boss. He is a big fan of your discoveries."

"The discoveries are a team effort. Anyone interested in the discoverers would need to meet Don and Ray too."

"That can be arranged."

In the black sedan leaving the farm FBI Special Agent Fife protested. "I still have a lot of work to do. You practically ruined any chance we had of getting to the bottom of the investigation."

"Agent Fife, you have completed your investigation of The Strongbox Foundation. I expect you will either be assigned to help find the real enemy, or be assigned another operation."

"What makes you so sure our bosses will see this your way?"

"My boss lives in a big white house."